# THE SKY WHALE

## P J MARSDEN

PJM

THE SKY WHALE

ISBN 978-0-9558227-1-1

Published by P J Marsden.

www.pjmarsden.com

A CIP catalogue record for this book is available from the
British Library.

Cover illustration by Karen Petrasko
Printed and bound by Copytech (UK) Ltd, Peterborough, UK.

For Edward

## *Chapter 1 – A Mysterious trail*

Have you ever seen something you just can't explain?

That happened to me once. I was on Round Hill looking up at the sky when I saw something incredibly weird.

I'd gone there to try out a helium balloon which I'd just bought through the internet. The balloon was climbing fast and the reel was spinning like mad as the line unwound. There must've been too much gas in it, or maybe a warm air current was helping to lift it up. I tightened the brake and slowed the reel down.

I was enjoying myself. It's great up on the hilltop in the middle of the moors, far away from everyone else – just me, the breeze and the clouds in the sky. Plenty of space to try out my kites, when it's windy, or balloons if it's calm. My granddad often used to take me there when I was younger.

I didn't have a father so granddad helped look after me. He was the one who taught me about balloons and things that fly, and explained why they go up instead of down. Some of his ideas seemed quite crazy, like the one about falling up.

'Imagine you are looking *down* at the clouds,' he would say, as we lay on our backs on top of the hill looking up at the sky. 'It's only gravity making you stick to the ground. If there was no gravity you'd fall right into those clouds.' It sounded weird at the time, but it's true if you think about it.

Sometimes we sent up balloons, big red party balloons that granddad filled with helium gas from a cylinder he carried in his rucksack. I'll always remember the very last time we went up Round Hill together. That day he passed the cylinder over to me.

'You fill them up this time, Danny,' he said. 'Let's see you do it.'

I fixed a balloon onto the nozzle and turned the knob. Gas hissed in. The balloon swelled and bobbed impatiently, eager to fly away. I tied the neck and gave it to granddad to hold, then I filled two more. When they were all ready to go I set them free, one after the other, and we watched the shiny red globes rise higher and higher till they dwindled away to tiny red dots high up in the sky. I sighed. The balloons, the day, everything was perfect.

But granddad seemed thoughtful. 'Danny, there's something different today, can you feel it?'

There *was* something different about the hill that day. The sky felt closer and I had a kind of dizzy feeling, like I didn't really know where I was. And something made me want to fly up after the balloons, up into the clouds.

'Yes, Granddad, I can feel it.'

'I've felt it before,' he went on slowly, 'on this hill. Round Hill's kind of special, I don't know why. There's something in the air. I've often wondered about it. But now I don't suppose I'll ever find out...'

He put his arm round me as we both gazed up at the sky. 'Maybe *you'll* find the answer one day, Danny.'

His words stayed in my mind, though I didn't really know what he was talking about. Soon after that he died.

My mum and I had a rough time at first. I really missed the kindly old man with his odd ideas and playful ways. But eventually things got back to normal, more or less. And now, some time later, here I was again, on a day that felt as dreamy as that final time with granddad, watching my big new silver balloon following the ghosts of the red ones up into the sky.

So far I was very pleased with my latest flying object. The balloon was carrying a weight of ninety pounds, but it could have carried much more. It was climbing steadily and the reel was whirring away. I kept my eyes on the shiny sphere and watched it getting smaller and smaller against the clouds.

That's when I saw a really strange sight. One of the clouds was slowly splitting in two. It looked as though something was pushing through the cloud, leaving behind a trail of clear blue sky. But I couldn't see what was doing it. I took out my binoculars to have a closer look but I still couldn't see what it was. At a guess it was as big as an airliner, but moving much more slowly. Something large and invisible.

Invisible?! I watched in amazement as the trail passed slowly through the cloud and out the other side. And that was all. I was totally baffled. What on earth could it be? I really wanted to know, but there was nothing more to be seen. A niggling mystery that would stay a mystery forever, I thought.

I turned my binoculars back to the balloon. It was close to the clouds and still rising; the reel was still clicking away. I put on the brake to slow it down and noticed there wasn't much line left. That meant it was around 3000 feet high. Over half a mile! I was well pleased.

Granddad would've been pleased too. I'd carried on going up to the hill and experimenting with balloons after he passed away, using the helium gas equipment and other stuff he'd left to me. Then I'd had this idea, a crazy idea that wouldn't go away. I kept thinking about it and planning how to do it. I bought some things with money granddad left me in his will: more helium gas, the special line, the hefty, shark-sized fishing reel and, finally, the big super-balloon.

I'd got the things ready in the shed in our back garden. I had to do it in secret because if my mother had found out she would've grounded me on the spot. What I was planning was really hare-brained; I was planning to go up into the air myself. In theory all I needed to do was fix myself to the balloon instead of the sack of rocks I'd used as a weight, and I'd be up and away.

In theory it was easy, but I have this problem; I don't like heights. I can't bear to look down from tall buildings. If I look over a balcony my legs go wobbly and the back of my neck gets icy cold. Funny, isn't it; a would-be flyer who's dead scared of leaving the ground. I really didn't know if I could do it.

But right now I had to carry on with the experiment. I stopped the reel and took hold of the line. There was quite a pull, and it was going to be a long and tiring job to reel the balloon all the way down again.

I was still holding the line when suddenly a weird feeling came over me. It gave me instant goose-bumps. Something awful was about to happen. My heart started pounding and my throat felt so choked I could hardly breathe. I had a vision of heaven and earth crashing together in one almighty bang and I seemed to hear a ghostly voice speaking words of dread.

*– The end... is nigh*

I felt sick with fear and very, very sad. What on earth was happening? Was I going mad? Then I heard a long mournful cry like the sound of a creature in distress. But I wasn't hearing the sound with my ears, I was hearing it inside my head. Where on earth was it coming from? It was something to do with the line! I jerked my hand away and straightaway the awful sounds and feelings disappeared completely.

Cautiously I reached out and touched the line again. I looked up towards the distant balloon. Once more the feeling of despair came over me and once more I heard the sorrowful cry. But this time the sounds seemed to be saying something, and ghostly words formed themselves inside my head.

– *Help... the end... help me... someone*

I wanted to help, I desperately wanted to help whatever was in such trouble. 'I'll help you!' I cried, though I didn't know what I could do.

– *Gratitude... hope-of-life*

The ghostly words were becoming clearer as I got more used to the strange way of communication.

– *Thank you... I give weight... bring me more... weighty things... please*

The line suddenly went slack. When I'd tugged on it earlier it had been stretched tight but now it was quite loose. My heart sank. Had the line broken? Had I lost my expensive new balloon? I turned my binoculars up to the sky. I saw a sudden swirl as the clouds mysteriously parted again. And there was my balloon, still in one piece and with the sack of rocks still slung beneath it.

But the whole contraption was dropping like a stone.

# Chapter 2 – Down to Earth

The balloon was falling fast. I couldn't understand it. Even if it was leaking gas it shouldn't be falling that quickly.

It was coming down further along the hilltop and I ran to meet it. I got there just in time to see the last stage of its descent. The balloon seemed okay but was falling incredibly fast, as though it was being dragged down by something much heavier than the sack of rocks I had used as a weight.

It hit the ground in front of me and I felt the thump through the earth. The sack split wide open with the force of the impact and the rocks spilled out onto the ground. With less weight to carry the balloon began to rise again. I quickly grabbed hold of the mooring rope dangling from the balloon, and groped for the quick release cord. I gave it a yank and gas gushed out of the valve. The balloon collapsed with a sigh.

I was completely baffled. What had gone wrong? Idly I picked up one of the stones that had spilled from the bag. I should say I tried to pick it up. I struggled to lift it. That chunk of granite shouldn't have weighed more than ten pounds, but now it was incredibly heavy.

I couldn't understand it. A third mystery, on top of the invisible shape and the voice in my head. Something odd was happening today, and I was bang in the middle of it.

But right now I didn't have time to figure it out. I had to get my things together. I had a big job to do, half a mile of line to wind up without getting it tangled. I slung the reel round my neck and began to follow the line over the ground, winding as I went.

My arm was aching by the time I'd reeled it all in. It was getting late and I was feeling cold and tired as I fetched my bike and loaded up. I bent down to pick up the super-heavy chunk of granite again, curious to find out more about it, but to my surprise it wasn't heavy any more. It felt like a normal piece of rock again.

By the time I'd ridden down the hill and across the moors it was starting to get dark. I stopped on a rise just before the village and checked to see if Walker and his goons were anywhere about. They didn't know where I disappeared to when I went up Round Hill, and I wanted to keep it that way. Take it from me, it's best to keep out of their sight.

The coast was clear. I carried on towards the village and soon reached my own house. I stowed all my gear in the shed and went inside.

'You're late tonight, Danny, ' said my mother, warming up my dinner. 'Been for a ride?'

She approves of me going cycling because of the exercise. Better than sitting in front of a computer all day.

I nodded. 'Yes, I went to the hill.' I couldn't tell her what had happened, because she didn't know about the big balloon.

After supper I got on with my homework. My biology project was due at the end of the week and I still had a lot to do. It was about parallel evolution, how different species evolve in the same way, like land animals going back to the sea millions of years ago, and changing to fish-shaped dolphins and whales.

But even while I did my work I kept thinking about the

strange events on Round Hill. Those mysterious words kept going round in my head – *'bring more weighty things'*. At the time I'd sensed something more than just words, I'd sensed what it was feeling; being dragged down, but struggling to stay up, like someone trying to stay afloat in the sea.

What was it? An alien UFO? Some kind of creature? How did it communicate like that? It had been very pleased when I helped it, whatever it was, and I could still feel the warmth of its gratitude. But what had I actually done? What had I done to help it?

Time passed slowly the next day at school. I was keen to get back on the hill, and impatient for the final bell to go.

'You're in a hurry, Danny,' said a voice behind me as I dashed towards the bicycle shed. It was Alison Day.

I stopped and waited for her to catch up. Alison is a new girl who started this term. Her father's the new Police Inspector for the town. She's very good-looking, brainy, brilliant at games, and I don't know why she gives me any time at all. But she seems to like talking to me and listening to some of my crazy ideas. And what could be crazier than my experience on the hill. The problem was, could I trust her to keep a secret? I was just making up my mind to tell her about it, when I had an unwelcome interruption. It was Walker.

'Hey Peterson, come here!' he yelled. He was with his two mates, Conway and Tucker.

I hesitated. I was busy and I had important things to do. The last thing I wanted now was hassle from Walker. But, as usual, I did what he wanted. I went over to him. He seemed to be in a fouler mood than usual. He stared at me through narrowed eyes, and leaned forward as though he was going to throw a punch.

'You're a pathetic nerd, Peterson,' he taunted. 'A waste of space. What are you?'

His mates grinned. I wasn't too worried because Walker never tried anything at school when there were other kids around. Then I noticed his eyes kept flicking in Alison's direction and I realised why he was after me. The moron was jealous. He didn't like to see me talking to Alison.

I returned his stare and recklessly raised an eyebrow. Walker's face twisted and he lifted his fist, but after a quick look round he decided against it. Instead he stuck his ugly face close to mine and lowered his voice. 'Peterson, you're dead!' he whispered menacingly.

I caught up with Alison, but she didn't want to talk anymore. She looked annoyed. 'Why do you let him push you around like that?' she demanded impatiently, then she hurried away without waiting for an answer.

I fetched my bike, feeling low. Walker had pushed me around all my life, ever since junior school, but I was bigger now and I knew I should stand up to him more. Alison's words had stung me.

So why did I let him do it? Because it was less painful than being caught outside the school by him and his two gorillas, that's why. I wasn't the only one they terrorised, but Walker had always picked on me specially, for some reason. Maybe he could tell that I never quite gave into him, not really, not inside my head. No matter how much he stamped on my toes or twisted my arm, I kept saying to myself *I don't care what you do.* But it still hurt.

Meanwhile, I had other things to think about. As I cycled home I started to plan the next balloon flight. Bring more weighty things, the voice had said. That must mean sending up another sack of rocks. But why? I felt a spot of rain and looked up. Grey clouds were scudding across the sky. Unfortunately the wind would be too strong to send up the balloon, but I decided to go to Round Hill anyway, in case I could see something.

When I got home I picked up a coat and binoculars then I set off again. Our road goes up as far as the moor then it turns into a gravel track that winds over the rolling moorland. You can see Round Hill in the distance, once you get over the first rise.

The hill is a rocky dome about 500 feet high. Imagine a big balloon of granite floating up through the surface of the earth, with only its top showing. According to granddad that's actually how those hills were formed, millions of years ago, when giant blobs of molten rock rose up through the earth.

As you follow the track up the hillside you pass a quarry, a section where the rock has been hacked away, like a bite taken out of a giant apple. It makes a cliff on that side of the hill. When you go onto the hilltop and look over the cliff, there's a straight-down drop of 200 feet. Scary.

It was quite cool up on the hill and I was glad of my coat. The week before I'd been caught in a heavy hail-storm without one. I found a sheltered spot among some boulders and settled down. I searched the clouds with my binoculars but could see nothing odd about them. No mysterious trails. The clouds were lower than the day before and moving quite fast. The creature, if it was still there, was probably higher up. I gazed at the sky and wondered if it could hear me. 'Hello, are you there?' I whispered, and waited for an answer. Nothing. I tried again.

Then suddenly I did feel something, a whisper of thought in my head so faint I could hardly hear it.

*– Help me...*

That was all, but it was enough. It hadn't just been a weird hallucination, there really was something up in the sky. And it still needed my help.

Suddenly I heard other sounds: the creak of bicycle pedals and the sound of voices. I was surprised. Usually I had the hill to myself. I peered out from behind the boulders and quickly ducked back again. Coming straight towards me were Walker and his two cronies.

## *Chapter 3 – Taking Off*

I crouched down behind the boulders, heart pounding, hoping they would keep going along the path without looking my way.

They stopped a few feet away and I heard Walker's loathsome voice. 'He must be somewhere round here,' he said. 'The little rat's going to get it this time. Find him!'

I was petrified. I was far from home and all alone with the town's worst bullies. Once they started searching properly they would find me for sure. And I didn't like to think what they would do when they found me. There were no witnesses out here on the moors. Then Tucker moved on and rode towards the cliff edge, overlooking the quarry.

'Hey, come look here,' he yelled, jumping off his bike.

The others followed him. Tucker dropped a rock over the edge and they cheered as it crashed down to the bottom. Then Walker found a big one and they all peered over the cliff to watch it fall. I could feel the thump as it hit the ground far below. The idiots cheered again. Then I heard Walker say: 'Splat! Just like Jason Blant,' and the others laughed.

I froze at those words. Jason Blant was a kid who fell from a multi-storey car park a few months before and broke both his legs. He was in a coma for two months, and when he woke up he couldn't remember how he had fallen. Hearing Walker talk like that sent a chill down my spine.

What if he and his gang had something to do with Jason's accident?

I watched the three secretly from my hiding place, knowing that they would soon start hunting me again. Tucker found another boulder, but it was too big for him to lift, so the three of them began rolling it towards the cliff edge. They had their backs to me. This was my chance!

I crept out and jumped on my bike just as they sent the boulder crashing on its way to the bottom. I pedalled furiously, expecting a cry at any moment. It wasn't long in coming.

'Hey, there's Peterson!' shouted Conway.

'Catch him!' yelled Walker.

I heard the clatter of their bicycles on the stony path behind me and took a quick look back. Walker was leading the way, a grin of hateful triumph on his face as he started gaining on me.

But I had the advantage. I knew the hill like the back of my hand, and I knew every twist of the treacherous track. I knew when you could race flat-out down the hillside and when you had to slow down for a curve in the path. I tore down the track, the others racing behind me. A curve was coming up that I knew was tricky. The path slopes the wrong way on the bend and the surface is loose and sandy. At the last moment I slowed down, veered outwards, then cut the corner.

Walker didn't make it. He raced after me without slow-ing and when he got to the bend he skidded, shot off the path and went bowling down the steep hillside. His mates stopped to watch as he bounced his way down the hill, desperately trying to stay on his bike. Finally he lost it completely and tumbled off. Brilliant!

I stopped a safe distance away and saw Walker get to his

feet then, feeling suddenly brave, I gave him a defiant wave and carried on home.

After supper I tried to work on my parallel evolution project. I was still investigating creatures in alien elements: rats that flitter through the night sky as bats, and birds such as penguins that can only fly underwater.

But I kept worrying about my problem, and in the end I switched off the computer and lay down on my bed to think it through.

The problem was this. After his stupid crash Walker would be after me more than ever before. Now that he'd discovered my getaway place on the hill, I couldn't take all my stuff up there again without major hassle from the gang. They'd mug me for sure and they'd wreck my precious balloon.

But I had to help the creature up in the sky. It was desperate. I couldn't go to the hill after school when Walker was free to bother me. So there was only one thing for it. I would have to bunk off school and go in the morning.

The next morning I woke up early and went outside to check the weather. Luckily the wind had died down and it was a calm day with only a few clouds.

Once my mother had left for work I went to the shed to get my things ready. The shed's really my workshop, quite large, where I keep my tools and bits and pieces, mostly inherited from granddad. I've got quite a collection of gadgets. I also keep the gas system there – the big cylinder that the helium comes in and a compressor for filling up smaller cylinders for the balloon. I found a stronger rucksack to replace the one that had split and filled up a fresh cylinder, then I loaded everything onto my bike.

I set off across the moor. I knew I'd get into trouble for bunking off school, but I didn't mind because I was happy to be helping the creature. I imagined how pleased it would be to see the sack of rocks coming up again.

I also found myself dreaming about Alison Day as I rode along; her sparkling blue eyes, long curly hair and the way she looked when she smiled at me. I really liked her. I wished she hadn't spoken to me like that. I suppose she thought I had no guts.

When I got to Round Hill I filled the rucksack with plenty of rocks and fastened it to the balloon. I anchored the reel to a massive boulder then I started to gas up. The balloon unfolded and swelled, rising up like a sleepy elephant, and began to tug at the rope holding the rucksack. I kept the gas hissing in, till the rocks began to lift off the ground, then I closed and sealed the valve.

At last the balloon was ready to go. Once again I watched the silver sphere disappearing into the sky above, and lifted my binoculars to track it better. The reel kept clicking away until finally all the line was out – 3000 feet.

I put my hand on the line and sent up a call. 'Hello, can you hear me?'

The creature's reply was very faint this time.

– *Greetings... friend*

'I've brought you more weighty things,' I called.

– *Where?*

'Same place.'

– *I see them... too far... cannot reach... no waves*

What did the creature mean? 'But you got there before,' I cried.

There was a pause. I started to get a picture in my mind of waves spreading downwards and then drawing back up again. Then my brain found a word to match the image – tide.

*– Tide... the tide different... come higher... you must come higher... I grow... tired*

The creature was desperate. I could feel how it was struggling, how much it needed to get away from the pull of the earth, like a whale going too close to shore and ending up helpless on the beach. My heart sank. I couldn't help the creature after all. I didn't know what to do. I had no more of the special line and the reel couldn't take more than 3000 feet anyway. I started to bring it down.

I reeled and reeled until the balloon was hanging a few feet above me. I gripped the mooring rope under my arms and unhooked the line. Then I loosened the heavy sack of rocks and reached for the gas release cord.

How stupid can you get. I should have done it the other way round. The rocks dropped to the ground, the balloon shot up and the gas cord swung away from me. The mooring rope was wrapped around me and I couldn't get it off in time. Seconds later I was fifty feet up in the air and rising, and it was too late to do anything about it.

# Chapter 4 – The Sky Whale

I scrabbled desperately for the loose end of the rope and managed to get a loop round my chest. I tied a double knot. Then I looked down.

Round Hill was straight below me. If I hadn't been so terrified, I would have enjoyed the bird's-eye view of my favourite hill, a dome of grey stone in a sea of green. As I rose through the air I began to see more of the surrounding countryside – the quarry, the track, and in the distance the town itself, complete with miniature houses, roads and the school I should have been in.

All the while I was desperately afraid of falling to earth. What if the balloon punctured? What if the rope broke? I wouldn't stand a chance. But they held up, and I after a while I stopped being so scared and even started to relax.

The balloon kept rising and I began to feel cold. Then it suddenly hit me. Falling to earth wasn't the problem. Going up was. I couldn't reach the cord to let out gas, and there was nothing to stop the balloon going up practically for-ever. And as I went up the air would get colder and thinner.

I was shivering even though I had a coat on. It was getting colder and colder. Soon it would reach zero, freez-ing point. Have you ever been in an airplane and seen the altitude and temperature shown on the movie screen? At 35,000 feet it's minus 40 degrees. When they dump the waste water they say it falls to earth as a block of dirty ice.

If I carried on the way I was going I'd turn into a block of ice myself. And the air would get so thin my eyes would want to pop out of their sockets. But they wouldn't be able to because they'd be frozen solid. At least it wouldn't be painful, I told myself. Long before I froze I would pass out through lack of oxygen.

Suddenly everything went white. For a moment I thought there was something wrong with my eyes, then I realised I was going through a cloud. Just as suddenly I came out into the sunshine again. I could see the cloud below me, like a carpet of cotton wool. And there, pressed into the layer of white, like a footprint on a sandy beach, was a shape. The imprint of a gigantic whale.

At least that's what it looked like. I couldn't actually see the whale, only the hollow shape of it pressed into the cloud. It seemed to have a big tapering body with a flat T-shaped tail and a flipper on each side of the body. I knew straight away that it was my creature, my invisible friend.

'Hello!' I cried. 'Hello, I'm here!'

There was a sudden swirl and the shape dissolved like a footprint washed by a wave. The creature's trace disappeared. Where was it? Had it flown away? I called again. 'Hello, over here!'

Suddenly I felt something brush against my legs and body. I reached out my hands and felt something soft and yielding. But it was completely invisible.

– *Greetings... friendship...*

As before the thoughts seemed to turn into words that I could hear in my head, only they were much clearer now.

– *Surprise... you are so... small... and dense*

The next words seemed almost shy, as though the creature was embarrassed to ask me.

*– Will you... will you... take weight?*

Take weight? That was exactly what I needed!

'Yes, give me weight!' I cried.

The creature pressed against me and I started to feel a curious sensation. It was like having someone breathe into your lungs and fill you up, only it was nothing to do with breathing. It was like being stuffed full of Christmas dinner, only it was nothing to do with eating. I felt a sensation of pressure behind my eyes, the kind you get when you hang upside down and the blood rushes to your head. It wasn't very nice. I was taking weight.

I felt myself moving down the creature's side and realised I was starting to descend. 'That's enough!' I cried. I didn't want to fall too fast.

*– Thank you... you are... generous and... unselfish*

I can't tell you how relieved I was to be drifting down towards the cloud again. 'Hope-of-life,' as the creature had said. I knew what that meant now.

'Thank you!' I called out to the empty air. I reached the cloud and everything went white again.

*– Come again... bring more weighty things... soon... please*

'Okay, I'll try,' I called back. Then I was through the cloud and looking down at the earth once again.

Round Hill had moved over to one side which meant that I was drifting further into the moors. I was shivering with cold, the rope was cutting painfully into my chest and my head was pounding from the extra weight in my body. But at least I was on my way back to the safety of solid earth. I watched the ground getting closer. There was something odd about it. The colours of the fields and trees seemed different from when I was going up; now the greens looked pale and washed out. I couldn't understand it.

Finally I came down on a grassy stretch. I landed with a jolt and fell over flat on my face. I struggled to push myself up but I couldn't move. It felt like I had weights strapped all over my body. As I lay pressed to the earth I felt another curious sensation, like I was emptying. It was like breathing out after you've been holding your breath, or having a pee when you've been bursting to go. It was the extra weight draining away.

The rising balloon helped pull me to my feet. Quickly I yanked the gas release cord, shrugged off the rope and looked around to see where I'd landed. I was on the open moor, miles beyond Round Hill. I had a long way to walk, I was chilled to the bone, and sore where the rope had cut into my chest. But I was alive and in one piece.

And the grass looked bright green again.

## Chapter 5 – A New Ally

I was still soaking in a hot bath when the front doorbell chimed. I jumped out and pulled on some clothes.

It was Alison Day at the door. 'Oh, sorry,' she said, staring at my bare feet, unbuttoned shirt and steaming wet hair.

'That's okay, come in,' I replied. I was surprised that she even knew where I lived. Now she seemed embarrassed.

'I just wondered how you were,' she said, dropping her eyes. 'Walker said you were too scared to come in. His face was a mess. Did you get in a fight because of what I said yesterday?'

I felt a bit embarrassed too, to have Alison in my home and no-one else around.

'No, actually we didn't fight, he fell off his bike,' I said, smiling at the memory of Walker flying down the hill. So he landed on his face, did he. Good.

She looked relieved. 'Why weren't you at school then?'

I looked her in the eyes. 'I had something to do,' I replied. 'Something that couldn't wait.'

'What was it?' She was curious now. 'What have you been doing?'

'I went up in the sky on a balloon. An invisible whale spoke to me and helped me get down again.'

She laughed out loud. 'Oh Danny, you are funny! A sky-whale! How do you think up things like that!'

'It's true. There's a creature up in the clouds. It needs my help. I've got to send rocks up there so it can lose weight...' I tailed off. It sounded crazy. It was crazy. But it was true.

Alison stopped smiling and looked at me seriously with her wide blue eyes. 'You can trust me, Danny. What's really going on?'

'It's true,' I repeated. 'I'll show you the balloon. I would've died up there if the creature hadn't helped me...' I started shaking. Delayed reaction was setting in. It had seemed so final at the time. I'd really thought I was going to die. 'Let me finish getting dressed,' I mumbled, and hurried out of the room.

I think Alison only started to believe me when we went out to the shed and she actually saw the balloon and the helium cylinders stacked against the wall.

'Look,' I said, showing her the mooring rope. 'This was tied round me.' I pulled up my shirt and showed her the livid red marks on my chest. 'Now do you believe me?'

She sucked her breath in. 'That looks awful! Okay, Danny, I believe you did go up and something strange did happen, but...' She stopped and shook her head.

'But you don't believe in the sky-whale,' I finished for her.

'Well, how could you see something invisible?'

'I saw the shape of it when it pressed against a cloud.'

'What is it? Where did it come from?'

I shrugged. 'I don't know. I don't think it should really be there. It's in trouble. It's sinking.'

Then I told Alison the full story, how I'd first heard the voice in my head, what had happened to the sack of rocks, my terrifying ordeal hanging from the balloon, what the sky-whale looked like and how the creature had made me heavier.

'It seemed grateful when I took the weight, like I was doing it a big favour,' I concluded.

While I was speaking I could see her disbelief melting away. The story was crazy but it made sense in a weird kind of way.

'It needs to lose weight,' she said thoughtfully, 'by transferring it to something else. How on earth can it do that...'

'I could feel the weight going in,' I ventured, 'and when I reached the ground it all seemed to run out again.'

'It's like electricity!' she exclaimed, 'but you were charged up with weight instead of electricity. When you were in the air there was nowhere for the weight to go. But when you touched the ground you were earthed and the extra weight drained away.'

'But why does the sky-whale need heavy things? Wouldn't it be better to send it something light?' I asked.

'Can't you see, Danny? Heavy things have more capacity. They can absorb more weight. It's like a big battery holding more electricity than a small one.'

I told you she was smart. 'Or think of a golf ball,' she went on eagerly, 'it's heavier than a ping-pong ball so it can store more momentum. That's why it goes further.'

I smiled back at her. It was a fantastic discovery, and it was terrific having someone like her to share it with. But there was still a problem.

'The first time, when I had the balloon on the line, the sky-whale could reach it, but now it can't anymore. It says the tide's gone out or something.'

'The tide? What do you mean, Danny?'

'I don't know, but it means I've got to get the rocks up much higher. Without using the line.'

'How are you going to do that?'

I took a deep breath. 'There's only one thing I can do. I've got to go up myself.'

'That's crazy!' cried Alison. 'You can't go up again. It's too dangerous!'

'I'll be alright.' I started to get out a few tools and things to work with. The balloon needed some changes before it could safely carry a passenger.

Alison started to say something, but she knew I'd made up my mind and I wasn't going to change it. 'Alright,' she said, 'then let me help you.'

I could use some help, I thought, and I liked having her around. I smiled. 'Okay, thanks.'

'What do you need to do?'

'I'll need a seat to sit in, and somewhere for a tank of helium, and I have to fit another valve. You could do the seat if you like.'

'Okay. How should I make it?'

I got out a spare rucksack. 'You could use this.' We figured out what to do and I showed her the tools she could use: my heavy-duty stapler, some nylon yarn, a Stanley knife, and other bits and pieces.

She gave me a generous smile. 'I didn't know you were such a whiz-kid, Danny. I'm impressed!'

It felt good to have her smiling at me. I smiled back.

We worked together on the balloon for the rest of the afternoon. Alison made a neat seat for me while I worked on the gas tank and valves.

'Do you want to try it out? ' she asked finally, holding it up.

She had opened up the sides of the rucksack and re-arranged the straps so it was more like a parachute harness, with a wide band going between my legs, fastening at the front. Strong straps supported me round my chest and under my arms. There were two ropes at the top to hang it from the balloon. I got into the seat, did up the straps, and then let Alison hoist me up, using a pulley on a rafter.

'How does it feel, Danny, alright?'

'Yes, it's great! Perfect!' I said, swinging gently. The seat felt secure and comfortable. It was going to work fine.

Alison was pleased. 'I think I'll just leave you hanging up all night,' she laughed.

'No you won't!' I undid the straps and scrambled down. 'Now we need a new sack for rocks.'

'Why do you need rocks, anyway, Danny? Can't *you* take the extra weight, like you did before?'

'No. Last time the sky-whale only gave me a little extra weight to make me come down. If it gave me any more I'd hit the ground too fast.'

I hadn't forgotten how the first bag had burst open when it hit the ground, or the jolt I'd had on landing with extra weight in me. Also, it didn't feel right to have the extra weight inside my body. I still felt fuzzy-headed, hours after my experience.

So we fished out another rucksack, and I showed Alison how I used granddad's old fisherman's scale – a kind of hook on a spring – to weigh the rocks.

'What should the sack weigh, Danny?'

I thought back to the time the balloon had dropped like a stone, and took a guess. 'I reckon the sky-whale doubles the weight of the rocks when it sheds weight. So forty pounds should be about right.'

I planned to dangle the sack on a rope ten feet below me. If we went down too fast the rocks would hit the ground just before me, and the balloon should then slow down. That was the theory. But would it work in practice?

When everything was finished we tidied up and went back into the house, just as my mother came home from work.

'Mum, this is Alison Day, Alison, my mother.'

'Hello Alison.' She shook Alison's hand and had a good look at her. I suppose she thought she was my girlfriend or something.

'Pleased to meet you, Mrs Peterson,' said Alison. 'Danny's been showing me his things in the shed.'

'You must come for tea one day,' said my mother, still trying to figure it out.

I blushed and shuffled uncomfortably. I wasn't some six-year-old who needed his mother to make invitations.

'Thank you,' replied Alison, with a mischievous glance in my direction.

'She seems a nice girl,' said my mother brightly, once she'd left. 'Very attractive.'

'Mm,' I replied.

# Chapter 6 – The Ocean in the Sky

It's funny how something important can suddenly make everything else seem trivial.

It didn't seem to matter that I was bunking off school for a second day, that I'd be getting into serious trouble for it, or even that Walker and his goons were after my blood. That was unimportant. The only thing that mattered to me was helping the sky-whale. It mattered to Alison too. She'd insisted on coming with me to help me get airborne. And, I suspected, to be there in case anything went dreadfully wrong, though she didn't like to admit it.

'Are you sure you want to do this, Danny?' she asked, when I was nearly ready to go.

I nodded. I was hanging below the balloon in the make-shift seat with a cylinder of helium at my side. I could feed more gas into the balloon through a plastic hose, if I needed to. The new valve I'd fitted would let out some gas when I pulled the cord, and shut again when I let go.

I was pleased with our handiwork. We'd worked hard to get it all together, and now it was time to put it to the test. But it was still scary. With pounding heart I gave Alison the signal to let go of the rope.

'Good luck!' she called, waving to me as the balloon began to rise. I waved back, and watched her upturned face get smaller and smaller, until she vanished to a dot on the shrinking grey summit of Round Hill.

It was a cool cloudless autumn morning. A slight breeze wafted the balloon to one side as it rose. I gave the release cord a tug just to make sure it worked, and heard a brief hiss of escaping gas. Good. The air got colder on my cheeks and I rolled down my woollen cap. I was wearing thick gloves this time and two jumpers underneath my coat. On my wrist was a sky-diver's altimeter which I'd bought some time before, only half-believing I'd ever be using it for real. And now I was.

I checked the dial. Already 4000 feet. The balloon was rising strongly even with the sack of rocks dangling below me on a rope. We'd put in extra gas so that the balloon wouldn't drop too quickly when the rocks got super-heavy. I reckoned it was time to call the sky-whale.

'Hello, I'm here!' I cried. After a few seconds I heard an answering call.

    *– Greetings... friendship... I struggle*

'Where are you?'

    *– Further out... keep coming... please*

I carried on rising and the air grew colder. The strange thing about being really high up was that I didn't feel afraid to look down. I suppose it was because the miniature fields, paths and trees looked more like toys than real things. I checked the altimeter again – 5500 feet. A mile high! No wonder it was so cold.

    *– Greetings*

The voice was loud and clear. The creature must be close. 'Where are you?'

    *– Puzzlement... do you not see me?*

Then I felt the sky-whale nudging against me.

    *– Take weight?*

'Give weight to the rocks, not me!' I cried. 'The weighty

things.'

    *– I give weight... relief... gratitude*

I felt myself moving against the sky-whale's side. The rocks had gotten heavier. I was going down, quite fast.

'Goodbye!' I called. 'I'll be back.'

    *– Farewell... thank you*

The air grew warmer and I looked down to see where I was. Round Hill was below me and over to one side; I would be landing further out on the moor. I looked for the tiny figure of Alison and gave her a wave, knowing she would be watching me through her binoculars. Then I concentrated on the landing. If all went well I wouldn't actually have to do anything.

The ground was getting nearer now, rushing up to meet me. I braced myself for the shock but at the last moment the sack of rocks hit the earth ahead of me and the balloon slowed down and stopped. Perfect! My feet didn't even touch the ground.

It took a few seconds for the weight to drain out of the sack of rocks into the earth, then the balloon began to lift up again. Brilliant!

It's great when a crazy plan works out okay, and all your doubts are behind you. I waved at the distant figure of Alison and saw her waving back. I felt like a hero. But I wasn't finished yet. Up and up I went, till the moor was far below me, and the cold was sharp on my cheeks.

I called out. 'Hello, are you there?'

    *– Greetings*

Once again I felt the creature brush against me.

    *– Take weight?*

'Give weight to the rocks. Not too much. I want to talk to you.' It's funny how quickly you get used to things. Like talking to something invisible.

> *– I give weight... thank you...*

The balloon lurched, then continued to rise more slowly.

> *– You went to the shore... and came back*

I laughed. 'I'm *from* the shore,' I replied, 'Where do you come from?'

A picture formed in my mind, of creatures swimming through shiny waves, also of glittering stars in a blue-black sky.

> *– I am from... the Ocean*

'What are you doing here? Are you in trouble?

> *– I came into this pool... on the last tide... I was trapped... I must wait until the next tide... I am too close to shore... and deathly heaviness seeps into me... but you are helping me...little one*

'When is the next tide?'

> *– When the... sun and moon are together ... But I need more lightness to swim out ... I cannot ride the waves... properly*

I was learning a lot, even if it was totally weird stuff. It was getting really cold and my throat was starting to get sore so I checked the altimeter again – nearly 7000 feet! We'd been rising faster than I thought.

'Give weight!' I cried. 'Give it to the rocks!'

> *– I give weight...thank you*

We started to descend. I looked down and had a moment of panic. I didn't know where I was. I couldn't spot Round Hill, not at first. Then I saw it way over to one side. Alison must be worried silly. Could the sky-whale nudge me in that direction? It was worth a try. I pictured the creature pushing me towards Round Hill.

'Please, push me that way.'

> *– You cannot use the waves? ... I will help you*

I felt something push me towards Round Hill, with a curious surging motion, like a boat cork-screwing through waves. I let the creature carry on until we were past the hill before I called out again.

'Okay, that's enough. Now give weight again.'

*– I give weight... thank you*

The sky-whale was very polite. I suppose giving and taking weight was very important to them. There was so much I wanted to know but I only had time for one more question. 'How much weight must you give?' I cried. 'How much lightness do you need?'

*– When close to shore... like this... need five, six times that each day... then more when tide comes in... to swim away*

As much as that. It would take us a lot of time and effort. 'I'll try!' I called. 'Goodbye!'

*– Farewell... thank you*

Three thousand feet and falling. The ground started rushing up to meet me. By luck or good judgment I was coming down right in the middle of Round Hill.

Would Alison try to catch the mooring rope, trailing alongside the sack? She didn't need to be told. She was already running to meet me. The sack landed at her feet and she quickly grabbed the rope.

'Danny, are you alright?'

'Thanks, I'm fine.' But actually the flight had left me exhausted and I was blue with cold. 'I'll take a break now.'

With the balloon safely tethered we sat down in the shelter of some boulders and unpacked our sandwiches and drinks.

Alison was excited and wanted to hear all about it. 'I saw the balloon coming back against the wind. Was that the sky-whale pushing it? What was it like?'

I began to tell her what the sky-whale had said, about the tides, the pool and the ocean where it came from.

'Danny that's fantastic! Where is it! Do you think people can go there?'

'I don't know. I got the impression the ocean was very high up.' I explained how the sky-whale was trapped in the pool until the next high tide.

'Sun and moon together,' she said thoughtfully. 'That must be when it's the new moon. That's next week some time, I think.'

A whole week. That would be difficult. I explained the problem to Alison.

'The trouble is, while the sky-whale is so close to earth it's slowly gaining weight. It said heaviness seeps in. So I'll have to keep skipping school to help it every day.'

We were in trouble already. Our school was tough on truancy and it wouldn't be long before they'd contact our parents to find out where we were.

Alison looked me in the eyes. 'I want to help you, Danny. I'll bunk off too. If you're prepared to get into trouble, so am I.'

I felt like giving her a hug but settled for a smile. Alison Day, model student, policeman's daughter, bunking school to help me. Or rather, to help the sky-whale. I was very glad to have her support.

'That'll be great, Allie.'

After our break we got moving again. I pulled on my gloves and got back into my seat while Alison checked the ropes.

'Pity I can't take up more rocks,' I said. Our invisible friend still needed a lot of help, and the limit was forty pounds a time.

Alison stopped what she was doing and her eyes

suddenly brightened. 'Maybe you could, Danny!' she cried. 'Do you think the sky-whale can take weight out of things, and make them lighter?'

'I dunno. Yeah, probably.'

'If it first took some weight out of you, it could dump more weight into the rocks, and you still wouldn't come down too fast.'

I didn't quite get it. 'But that only moves the weight around,' I objected. 'How does that help the sky-whale?'

Alison beamed at me. 'That's true the first time, Danny. But if you don't actually touch the ground when you come down you should stay light. The next time you go up the sky-whale won't need to take weight from you.'

I got it. It was a brilliant idea. With me being lighter, the sky-whale could dump more of its weight into the rocks, and I'd go down at the same speed.

But could the sky-whale really make me lighter? We couldn't wait to see. Alison put another twenty pounds of rocks into the sack to absorb the extra weight, while I let more gas into the balloon.

Soon we were ready. Alison gave me a final wave as she let go the mooring rope, and I was on my way.

I watched the earth fall away, and marvelled at what I was doing. I was doing what I had so often dreamed of, flying up into the sky. I still found it nerve-wracking, but not as terrifying as I'd once expected. I'd got through my fear by focusing on the sky-whale, and now I was okay.

But things could still go horribly wrong. The balloon might split or a valve might leak, or a carelessly tied knot might come loose. Then *I'd* be the one falling to my death, not the sky-whale.

The air grew colder and I checked the altimeter – 5000 feet. It was time to call the sky-whale.

'Hello, are you there?' I didn't know its name. Did they have names? There was still a lot we didn't know about the creature.

> – *Greetings... you are saving me... from deathly heaviness ... thank you little one...*

The creature seemed to be speaking more clearly now, or perhaps it was just my own brain fitting more words to its thoughts. I told it what to do.

'Give weight now, but not much. I want to stop moving.'

The sky-whale understood. It gave the rocks just enough weight to halt my ascent.

'Now listen. Can you take weight from me?

> – *Yes... I will take weight... if you need*

'I want you to take weight from me, then put it in the rocks. Can you do that?'

> – *Yes*

I waited. The sky-whale waited.

> – *Puzzlement... will you give weight?*

'I don't know how. Can't you do it?'

The creature seemed amused.

> – *You are like a new calf... I can do it... but I will show you how... first I give weight to you...*

Once again I felt that strange sensation, like something filling me up. I had the same feeling of pressure as before, but this time it was more intense.

> – *Now push it out... quickly*

I pushed against the pressure with some part of me that I'd never used before. Then I felt the sky-whale helping me by sucking out the extra weight. I pushed hard and the sky-whale sucked, and all of a sudden I'd given back all the extra weight and more.

It felt like I'd emptied my lungs and then breathed out

more, only it was nothing to do with breathing. I'd given weight! I was lighter. It felt strange, a nice feeling, kind of relaxed and dreamy. The air, which had been freezing cold, now felt pleasantly warm on my skin. But the strangest, most amazing thing of all was what I could see.

I could see the sky-whale.

## Chapter 7 – Seeing the Sea

I could see the sky-whale right in front of me. It was big.

As the balloon began to pull me higher the creature slowly dropped away, and I was able to get a better view of it. It was large, it was definitely whale-shaped and it was quite transparent. I could see the fabulous creature but I could also see right through it.

It was as big as the biggest earth whale, with a long tapering body, two side flippers and a wide flat tail just like a real whale's. The creature surged up level with me again, and looked at me. Its placid, wise face was a bit like a dolphin's, only much bigger.

*– You need more lightness?*

I gazed into a gigantic round eye, big as a saucer.

'Thank you, no. I can see you now!'

Its skin glinted with shifting reflections, like the surface of a soap bubble. Inside the great beast I could just make out the outlines of some inner structures. Bones, I supposed, and other internal organs.

I felt different. Everything was different. The air felt as warm as a summer's day. And there were shimmers of light in the air, coming and going almost too fast to see. I looked up, down, all around. The air was clear and I could see for miles, but when I focused in a certain way I could just make out glints of light coming towards me from every direction. And each time they passed around me I felt a little push, like the surge of a wave. These were the waves the sky-whale had talked about.

Suddenly something flashed in front of me. A school of tiny fishes flew past my startled eyes. I looked around and saw a transparent jelly-fish, as big as an umbrella, flapping lazily by, and here and there some transparent sponge-like objects floating in the air.

The sky-whale was coming up to me again. It seemed worried.

*– You are going too far... there is danger... above...*

I checked my altimeter – 9000 feet!

I hadn't even noticed it. By now I should have been gasping for breath through frozen lips, but I wasn't. I had no trouble breathing and it still felt like a warm summer's day.

'Give weight!' I cried. 'Not to me, to the rocks!'

It seemed funny to be telling such a large creature what to do. I must have seemed like a tiny pilot-fish next to its great bulk. All the same, I was the one creature able to help the sky-whale, because I could go down to the earth and back again.

The balloon started to fall, around its usual speed, so I reckoned the rocks were about twenty pounds heavier and I was the same amount lighter. Just what we'd planned!

I looked down. The ground below looked different. All the colours were deeper. The fields were dark green and the rocky top of Round Hill was nearly black. Losing weight changed the way I saw things.

At 5000 feet the sky-whale guided me into position above the hill. It seemed to know exactly what to do.

*– Farewell ... the shore is close ... take care*

At 4000 feet I noticed a change. I was coming out of the waves. The glints of light were fainter, their ghostly touch much lighter. I carried on falling, then looked upwards again. I couldn't make out individual waves any more, but I could see an area of sky above me that seemed lighter than the rest.

That must be the sky-whale's ocean, I realised. Or, rather, the pool that the poor creature was trapped in. From below I couldn't see how high up it stretched. I'd gone nearly two miles up and I'd seen no end to the waves. It probably went much higher than that. Five, six miles? And above the pool, what? The ocean?

Alison started running towards me as I neared the ground. The sack of rocks struck the earth hard, while I stayed dangling in the air. She stopped and called out in astonishment. 'Danny! You look like a ghost! What happened?'

I was dying to tell her, but there wasn't going to be time. The sack had already lost its extra weight and the balloon was starting to rise again.

'Allie, I could see it. The sky-whale. It's fantastic!' I yelled, but the balloon pulled me up and away.

Now that I was lighter the balloon lifted the extra rocks with ease. Our plan had worked! For the rest of the day the sky-whale could dump sixty pounds each time.

I will always remember that first amazing day I became lighter; the dreamy feeling, the mysterious waves, being able to see the sky-whale face to face. And there were lots of questions to be answered.

'Are there more of you?' I asked. 'How many sky-whales are there?'

I got a mental picture of creatures on the move, a steady stream of sky-whales, big and small, gliding gracefully through the air.

> – *There are sixteen in my... family group...hundreds of us travel together... and thousands more... across the ocean*

'Where do you go to?'

> – *We follow the waves... we follow the food... we count the stars...*

I got a mental picture of glittering stars in an indigo sky, while far below lay the earthly continents, blue seas, and oceans of white cloud.

> – *We go to and fro... we follow the sun*

Seasonal migration. Processions of sky-whales travelling from pole to pole, high in the sky, completely invisible to everyone down below.

'How did you get trapped in this pool?'

> – *Embarrassment... I was foolish... I went close to shore for some...*

A picture of a towering cumulus cloud and tons of little white balls flying up on a thermal. Hailstones!

> – *hailstones ... because I sought... extra lightness... for my new one... I stayed too long*

I saw the sky-whale swooping down to revel in the hailstorm, shedding pounds of weight as millions of icy grains drummed against its sides, but staying too long, and discovering that the way back to the ocean was closed.

'When will it open again?'

> – *Five more days...*

I got a picture of a thin crescent moon, set in a dark blue sky, showing when the tide would be stronger.

> – *It will be my last chance... the tide will not be this strong again... until next spring... sorrow... my family will move on... without me... and I shall perish*

It was an awful prospect. We just had to keep the sky-whale safely afloat until the ocean waves reached down to her. But could we do it? Could we really keep going for five more days and nights? It seemed impossible, but we had to try.

I lost track of time. The afternoon passed in a dream as I kept dropping down to earth, dumping the extra weight and soaring up again to the sky and the waves. Each time I went up I stayed as long as I could. Being lighter made me feel kind of elated, on a high, and while I was feeling like that I wanted to be up with the sky-whale, not down on the ground.

Eventually I had to stop. Time was passing. I'd not been steering back to Alison on the hilltop, but had been landing wherever the balloon drifted. But now it was time to return to Round Hill, and stop for the day. The sky-whale was in good shape as I said goodbye.

   *– Farewell...I shall be free of danger... until*
     *tomorrow... grateful...*

It pushed me toward the centre of the hill and gave weight to the rocks for the last time.

'Goodbye!'

I drifted down, but kept looking up at the sky, at the faint shimmering shape swimming alone in its mysterious aerial pool.

Alison came running to meet me, and grabbed the mooring rope. 'Danny, you've been so long!'

I let out some gas and sank down to touch the ground. I felt weight flooding up my legs from the earth, filling me up once more. The grass stopped being so green and the rocks turned from black to grey again. I looked up. I could no longer see the sea in the sky. It was invisible once more, and so was the distant sky-whale.

'Hello Allie, I...' I sat down dizzily.

'You left me on my own, all this time!' She didn't sound too pleased with me. It was four o' clock already.

'I'm sorry,' I said, still feeling hazy. 'I wasn't thinking. I was in the waves. It was so weird.'

'Danny, are you alright? What happened?'

I told her the story: how I was able to see the sky-whale, the other sky-creatures, the mysterious waves that seemed to go through me.

'I went nearly two miles up and I didn't feel cold at all! And I could still breathe perfectly well. It felt great.'

I told her about the sky-whale's migration with its family and the hailstorm that had tempted the creature to come down and stay too long. And now it was in serious trouble trapped in the pool. The channel from the pool up to the ocean was getting shallower.

'The last big tide of the year is on Tuesday,' I said anxiously. 'That'll be the sky-whale's last chance to get free. Otherwise...'

Alison had calmed down. She patted my arm. 'Don't worry, Danny, we'll do it somehow.'

I nodded. We had to.

'Now tell me about being light. What does it feel like?'

I stood up. 'Come here, I'll show you.'

She came forward curiously and I put my arms round her. I concentrated, trying to draw weight from her. 'Can you feel anything?' I asked. I thought I knew how to do it, but it didn't seem to be working.

'Danny! What are you doing!'

I blushed. 'Sorry, I was only trying to show you. I don't think it works on the ground.'

'That's okay, I'll find out what it's like. I want to go up

myself tomorrow.'

I was dumbstruck. There was no way I could let Alison take the risk, but I didn't know what to say. I began letting the gas out. When the balloon was empty and flat on the ground I ventured a cautious reply.

'Alison, listen, I don't think you should go up.'

'Why not?' she demanded.

'It's too dangerous.'

'It's the same for me or you, what's the difference?'

'Yeah, but...'

'I suppose it's because I'm a girl.' Her eyes challenged me to deny it.

'I know how to work it,' I said defensively. I didn't want to see Alison flying up forever, or dropping to the ground like a stone.

'Well, I can learn! Honestly, I can't see the problem.'

'The sky-whale knows me. You might not be able to tell it what to do.'

'You're all the same! You don't think girls can do anything!'

'But if anything happened to you...'

She gave me a glare. 'I'm going up!'

Then I said something rather dumb. 'Well it's my balloon and I won't let you!'

'Don't be so frigging childish!' she cried, and pedalled away before I could stop her.

'Alison!' I gazed at her disappearing figure with heavy heart. A marvellous day had suddenly gone wrong, and it was all my fault.

I carried on packing up alone. I folded the balloon, emptied the sack of rocks and coiled up the ropes. Finally everything was safely stowed away on the carrier. I started cycling down the track, still brooding about my stupid quarrel with Alison.

I was also starting to worry about my helium supply back home. The big cylinder in the shed must be getting low with all the gas I'd been using, and I didn't actually know how much was left. So as I rode along, I wasn't thinking about school being out already, or anyone else being around.

I was down the slope and just passing the quarry, when I noticed some figures in the distance coming towards me. I slowed down. It was two of Walker's gang, and I didn't want to meet them. I needed a place to hide before they saw me. But where?

At the foot of the cliff there's an old hut that the workmen used to use. I sped towards it across the bumpy quarry floor. The hut was made of granite slabs with a metal roof and door. I slid the bolt open and pulled my bike inside. Then I quickly shut the door again. I peeped through the tiny window.

Tucker and Conway were just cycling up the track. 'I saw him, I tell you,' said Conway. They stopped and looked around.

'What about that hut,' said Tucker. He started to come towards it.

Suddenly the hut didn't seem such a good idea. I would've had a better chance out on the moor. The door clanked open.

'He's here!' yelled Tucker triumphantly.

I grabbed a pick-handle that was lying with some tools, and raised it like a baseball bat. 'You want something?' I said firmly, trying to sound tough, though my heart was pounding like a hammer.

Tucker was startled. He hadn't expected his victim to

fight back. He slowly backed away.

'Lock him in!' cried Conway. 'Then we can go get Walker.'

The door clanked shut and I heard the bolt slide home. The window opening had no glass, but it was covered by a metal grill. There was no way out.

# Chapter 8 – Running out of Gas

I heard the two goons talking gleefully outside the hut.

'You wait here and see he doesn't get away,' said Tucker.

Tucker was the worst of the two, a vicious psychopath like Walker. Once in a careers class he said he wanted to be a hangman when he grew up. I could see him making a good torturer actually. Conway was a weaker character, a bit of a dim-wit who did what the other two told him. His career would probably be as a convict in prison, caught for doing someone else's dirty work.

I heard Tucker rattling away on his bike, and peeped out of the window again. He was just disappearing down the track. It would only be a few minutes before he returned with Walker. I shuddered to think what would happen when they came back. Lately Walker seemed to be getting more vicious than ever before, if that was possible. Now he would feel like murdering me, after his painful crash.

I quickly went round the hut, looking for some way out, or something I could use. There were only a few old tools, a broken oil lamp and a shovel. I went back to the window. Conway was standing outside the door, picking his nose. I checked the window grill again. It was firmly fastened with four solid bolts. But luckily the bolts were on the inside of the grill, where I could reach them. And I'd noticed a spanner among the old tools. I looked for Conway again. He was still outside the door, groping in his pocket for something. He pulled out a tin of tobacco and started to roll a cigarette.

'Hey, Conway, give us a smoke,' I pleaded.

'Sod you!' he replied.

'I had a packet myself but I left them up the hill,' I went on pathetically.

Now he was interested. 'Where?'

'In that clump of boulders near the edge of the cliff. If you fetch them for me I'll give you one.'

I could see his mind working. Slowly. He grinned. 'Sure I'll fetch them.'

As soon as he was gone I set to work. Out came the four bolts, out came the grill, out climbed Danny Peterson. I opened the door and hauled out my bike. Then I quickly replaced the grill and closed and bolted the door again. I was free.

There is a second way back to the village. If you go along the foot of the cliff to the other end, you meet a disused road that the trucks used to run on. I cycled as quietly as I could across the quarry floor and onto the road. Then I sped off homewards.

I was going the long way round but I didn't mind. I was laughing. I kept thinking of Conway searching for non-existent cigarettes, then returning to stand guard over a non-existent prisoner. And I kept thinking of Walker's face when he found his promised victim gone. I wasn't the one who'd get hammered that day.

When I got home the first thing I did was to phone Alison.

'Hello Alison.'

'Yes?'

'Listen, I'm sorry, I shouldn't have said what I said.'

'Danny, I thought we were doing this together. I was really enjoying it...'

'I know, me too. I mean with you...'

'Danny, I still want to help you. I think you were incredibly brave to try out the balloon like that.'

'Well, I ...'

'But I do want to go up myself. Otherwise I won't ever see the sky-whale!'

'Okay. But I'm still a bit worried about what it might do. It doesn't know you. So I think we should go up together the first time.'

I could hear her smile over the phone. 'That'll be great, Danny! Thanks.'

'I'll go and make another seat right now,' I told her.

'Great! Thanks Danny. Bye!'

I went out to the shed, feeling good. But then I checked the dial on the big helium tank to see how much gas was left. My heart sank. It was much lower than I'd thought, not even enough to fill the balloon properly one more time.

I called the gas company straightaway. Luckily they delivered to our area every Friday, and there was still time to order for the next day. But could I get the money in time?

I switched on my computer and checked my bank account. Fifty pounds. I needed a lot more than that.

I did have some more money in another account which Granddad had left me, but I was only allowed to spend it if my trustee, Mr Spinks, agreed. He's a lawyer who looks after my trust fund. I was supposed to use it for computers and educational things. Did that include saving sky-whales?

I knew that Granddad would have approved. He'd guessed there was something odd about Round Hill, and he'd hinted that I might solve the mystery one day. He would've gone up in the sky himself if he could.

I picked up the phone and called Mr Spinks.

'Hello Danny, what can I do for you?

'Hello Mr Spinks.' I tried to sound grown-up. 'I need some more of my money for a project I'm working on. It's going very well but I've run out of helium and I've got a deadline.'

'How much do you need, Danny?'

I took a deep breath. 'Four hundred and fifty pounds. I have to buy a quantity at a time.'

'That much! You know the money's really supposed to be for educational things.'

'Yes I know, Mr Spinks. I actually need the helium for that gas equipment Granddad left me. It's run out.'

'Mmm. Alright then, I'll see about a transfer.'

'Could you do it tonight, please, on the internet?'

'Afraid I can't do that, Danny. The money's in a thirty-day account. You'd lose interest. I'll give notice tonight, but you'll have to wait a month for it to come through.'

There was nothing I could do. I thanked him and said goodbye. How on earth could I get £450 by ten o' clock the next morning? Apart from my inheritance we're not very well off, and my mum couldn't lend me the money even if she wanted to. I couldn't ask her anyway. We were sunk.

I couldn't bear to think about the sky-whale. When morning came it would be anxiously waiting for me, but I wouldn't be coming. Not then, nor the next day, nor the next. What happened when sky-whales fell to earth? Now I wouldn't even be able to ask the creature, that or any other questions.

I called Alison to tell her the bad news. 'We're low on gas, and I can't get more money in time,' I said bleakly. 'Not straightaway. I'm £450 short. We won't be able to go up any more.'

There was a long silence. 'Hello Allie, are you there?'

Yes Danny. I'm thinking.' She kept her voice low. 'Listen, I think I can help with the money.'

My heart rose. 'How?'

'I've got some money in a savings account,' she explained quickly. 'It's supposed to be for our next family holiday. I'll get into real trouble if I spend it, but I don't care. We've got to carry on.'

'Are you sure? I need an extra £450. Have you got that much?'

'Yes, I've got a bit more.'

'Great!' I nearly collapsed with relief.

'And guess what. I've got my own seat for the balloon. It's a harness from my dad's boat. I'll bring it round in the morning.'

'Allie that's fantastic!' She had completely saved the day.

We arranged to meet at her bank the next morning, then I called the gas company and confirmed the order. One large cylinder of helium for Mr Peterson, price £498, cash on delivery.

My mother came in as I put the phone down. 'Hello Danny, how was school today?'

I blushed guiltily. 'Okay,' I mumbled. I suppose school had been okay for everyone who actually went. But not for me and Alison.

Somehow we had to keep bunking off for three more school days without the alarm being raised. I didn't care about what happened after that. The telling off, detentions and extra homework were in the future. What we had to do first was far more important.

We had to save a beautiful creature which was trapped and lonely, swimming desperately round and round in the pool above our heads.

## Chapter 9 – Alison Takes Off

The next morning my mother was still in her dressing gown at eight o' clock when I came down.

'I've got the morning off,' she said cheerfully. She was relaxing with a cup of coffee in front of the telly.

My heart sank. The helium would be arriving at ten o' clock and I had to be there to receive it. Should I say I was sick and stay at home? What about going to the bank?

Then she got up. 'Have you finished in the bathroom? It's a lovely morning. I think I'll go into town soon.'

Whew! But because she was still at home at eight-thirty I had to get dressed in my school clothes and pretend I was leaving for school.

I didn't go anywhere near our school. Instead I rode round and round the back streets until nine o' clock. Then I went to my bank and drew £50 from the machine. I quickly rode back to the back streets. By now any nosy teachers should be in school already, but my mother would be somewhere around town, and she was the last person I wanted to bump into.

At nine-thirty I met Alison outside her bank just as the doors were opening. We hurried inside and got on with our business. Everyone seemed to be staring at us. I exchanged a secret glance with Alison while the clerk was preparing the cheque for the gas company. No-one, but no-one could have guessed what we were really up to.

'Thanks Allie, I'll pay you back,' I whispered. She gave me a smile.

We only relaxed when the cheque was finally in her hand. We were going to be alright. Now all we had to do was get back home in time for the delivery.

We were just turning off the main road when a car went by that I recognised, a green Rover with a 'Keep your distance' sticker on the back bumper. It was Mr Grayson, the headmaster. We raced round the corner and the car carried on without stopping. Had he seen us? I wasn't sure. We hurried home. The gas delivery truck was pulling up outside my house. We were just in time.

We helped the delivery man get the big cylinder round the back on his trolley. It was quite a job. It's funny to think that gas can be so heavy, but when it's compressed that's what happens. I signed for the gas and gave the man his cheque. Four hundred and ninety-eight pounds.

'Thank you,' he said and looked at us curiously. 'Have fun!'

We filled up a small cylinder and loaded the balloon and the rest of the stuff onto my bike. Then we made some sandwiches and packed a couple of drinks. Finally we were ready to go. Ready to carry out our craziest plan yet.

When we got to the hilltop we assembled our gear very carefully. What we had to do was quite complicated because we were going up together, and the balloon couldn't take both our weights combined.

First I had to go up alone to the sky-whale, to lose some of my body weight, taking two bags with 40 and 20 pounds of rocks. They would pull me down again once they had gained extra weight. When I touched down Alison would have to hook herself onto a rope while I stayed hanging in the air. Then I'd untie the larger sack of rocks and we'd both go up. That was the plan.

I got the ropes ready including a new one with a pulley gadget. Alison worked in silence, with an anxious frown on her face. She put on her harness and pulled the straps tight, checking everything carefully. There would be no second chances up in the air. At last we were ready. The balloon had been filled to its maximum and was straining to go.

I gave Alison's arm a pat. 'See you soon. Don't worry, it'll be alright.'

She managed a smile. 'Okay, see you soon.'

Then I climbed into my seat and checked the gas valves one more time. Everything was ready. 'Okay!' I called.

Alison let go the rope and waved me away. I could see she was still tense. Next time it would be her turn.

The balloon rose steadily through the morning air. It was another cool day and I passed through a cloud on the way up. I thought back to that first trip, which seemed so long ago now, and how lucky I'd been to spot the sky-whale pressed against the cloud, just in time. We'd saved each other from certain death that day.

The air grew colder. At 5000 feet I sent out a call. 'Hello, I'm here!'

    *– Greetings... I see you... come higher*

I carried on. Soon I felt the magical creature brush against me.

'Hello. Are you alright?'

    *– I have lightness... I ride the waves*

'That's good. You can give more weight today, but first will you take weight from me?'

The sky-whale pressed close.

    *– You must try to do it... little one*

I concentrated, trying to push weight out, but it was no good. I couldn't do it by myself.

'Can you show me, please.'

– *Like this... I give weight... you give weight*

I pushed hard and the extra weight whooshed out as the sky-whale sucked it in, and suddenly I was light again. Once again the air was warm, the sky-whale swam in front of my eyes, and ghostly waves rushed past me. I remember-ed my manners. 'Thank you,' I said.

Now to fetch Alison. The sky-whale guided me carefully above the hilltop and gave weight to the rocks. Down I sank. Alison ran to meet me. She quickly hooked her harness onto the rope and began heaving herself up on the pulley. Soon she was hanging alongside me.

'Okay?' I asked.

She nodded. I tugged at the slip-knot to release one of the sacks. Would the balloon have enough lift for the two of us? It was touch and go. The balloon hung uncertainly for a second, then it made up its mind and began to rise. Alison swung by my side as we drifted slowly upwards. I was glad to be with her on her first trip. I knew just what she was feeling, excited but scared, and it made me feel the same, all over again.

We must have been mad. Imagine, two kids, hanging precariously below a balloon that wasn't really designed to lift people, intending to fly a mile or more up in the air, when all sorts of things could go wrong.

Alison couldn't bear to look down at first, but after a while she got used to it. I kept looking up, willing the sluggish balloon to rise faster. I could see the sea above us, a lighter area of sky where the mysterious waves glinted as they moved to and fro.

'It's cold, isn't it!' shivered Alison. She had two red spots on her cheeks.

I reached out for her hand and held it tight. She was freezing. Then something odd happened.

'That's better. I feel warmer!' she cried.

And I felt a bit cooler. I knew what that meant. Half my lightness had drained into Alison. We both had some now.

'Look up. Can you see anything?' I asked.

'I don't know,' she said uncertainly. 'It looks brighter.'

'That's the waves! You'll see them better once you lose more weight.'

She was looking at something higher up. 'Is that... I can see it, Danny, it's the sky-whale!'

She had sharp eyes, for the creature was very nearly invisible. I could only just make it out. The sky-whale was waiting for us.

   – *Greetings*

'I heard it!' cried Alison. 'I heard it speak!'

   – *You are the mate?*

'Er, sort of,' Alison replied.

   – *Welcome*

'She wants to help too,' I said. 'Can you take weight?'

   – *I take weight*

Then, with me and Alison holding hands, the sky-whale nudged against us, and I felt the peculiar sucking out feeling once more. Suddenly the air felt nicely warm again, and the touch of the waves more substantial.

Alison gasped. The sky-whale was revealed in all its glory.

'You're supposed to say thank you for taking weight,' I whispered.

'Thank you!' she cried, and she meant it. 'You're beautiful!'

A big eye regarded us curiously. Rainbow reflections chased over a vast transparent body, and a great tail swished gently in time with the waves. The balloon began to climb faster, and as we rose the sky-whale rose beside us. It seemed to be thinking.

    *– You are young ones?*

'Yes, we are,' replied Alison. 'How old are you?'

    *– Eighty-five turns of the large planet*

What did that mean? It would have to wait.

Alison was studying the creature carefully. 'You're female, aren't you.'

    *– Yes. So are you... I think*

'Yes. What's your name?'

    *– Thundera*

'I'm Alison, and this is Danny.'

I felt left out. Trust the girls to sort out the basics. I checked my altimeter. Nearly 7000 feet. We were going too high. Thundera seemed to be getting nervous too. She rose above us, circled round, then sank down again.

    *– You are too far out ... danger*

'Then come and give weight,' I called. The sky-whale swam nearer and brushed against me. I felt the weight flowing in, and the air turned icy on my cheeks. I gasped at the shock. I'd gotten careless about high altitude. But we were falling again, and soon the air would become more tolerable.

'Allie, I'm normal again. Don't touch me or you'll lose your lightness!'

She nodded. 'Okay.'

I did a double-take. Alison's face looked pale and washed out, like a ghost. 'Are you okay?'

'Yeah, I'm fine!' she laughed. 'It's fantastic. I feel kind of dreamy.'

I looked around for Thundera but now she was invisible to me. I called out for her. 'Thundera, steer us to the hill, please.'

While the sky-whale was nudging us towards the hilltop I went over the controls with Alison one more time.

'If you can't come down, let out the gas a bit at a time. Here's the string for the valve.'

'Okay. And if I want to go up do I turn on the cylinder?'

'That'll only work if you're falling slowly. The balloon's nearly full already. If you're falling too fast you'll have to undo the bags and let them fall.'

'Okay.'

What a team. Danny Peterson, flying instructor, with two days' experience. And Alison Day, going solo after ten minutes' training. When we landed I slid down the rope and hauled the balloon over to where we'd dropped off the first sack of rocks. Now the sack would take my place. I hooked it onto the rope. 'Okay?' I called.

Alison grinned down at me. 'Okay, I'm ready. You look really weird Danny.'

I smiled back as my pale friend began to rise, though my heart was in my mouth. She looked so precarious hanging on the rope, like a mountaineer dangling over a drop. Except that her drop would be a whole mile down.

'Bye Allie!' I called, though I don't know if she could still hear me. 'Take care!'

## Chapter 10 – Troubles in the Sky

I went back to our sheltered spot between the boulders and sat down with the binoculars. Now it was my turn to watch and wait. I tracked the balloon going up between the clouds and thought how Alison must be feeling. It had been fantastic to share the dreamy lightness with her, and feel those waves wash past us. It was right that she was going up too. And Thundera liked her, I could tell.

That day there was no stopping Alison. She went up and down three times to dump weight for the sky-whale, and each time she stayed up for ages. Talking, I could guess. When she finally did land back on the hilltop she was in a daze. She clung onto me as I steadied her.

'Danny, I feel... it was fantastic...'

We sat down together. 'How did it go? How's Thundera?' I asked.

'She's fine. Do you know where they came from?' Alison was dying to tell me. 'They came from down here, Danny, from the earth, that's what she told me!'

'From here?'

'They've got a story about the beginning of the world. A long time ago when the moon was closer to the earth the levity waves were strong all the way to the shore.'

'Levity waves?'

'Oh that's just what I call them. Opposite of gravity,' she said airily. 'That's how they swim. The waves push them wherever they want to go.'

'Go on.'

'Well, a long time ago their ancestors on earth learned how to give weight and ride the waves. The two things go together, obviously.'

I looked at her blankly.

'Danny, getting lightness is the key to everything! When you lose weight you sort of shift to where you can feel the waves. You go halfway to another dimension, I guess.'

'Anyway, they gradually learned how to do it properly. Not just the sky-whales, all sorts of animals, and also plants.'

'They spent more and more time up in the air. Their food was also flying around by then so that's how they managed.'

'When the moon moved further away from the earth the levity waves moved away from the shore too. Now there's a gap between the earth and their ocean, where nothing can swim. If they drop out of the waves they sink to earth.'

'Did they came from the land or the sea,' I asked. 'I mean, did the sky-whales evolve into whales up there, or were they already whales when they left.'

'I don't know, Danny. She talks about the sea so they probably evolved from sea whales. But I don't think they really know themselves. It's like a myth. It was such a long time ago.'

It was an amazing story. And something told me we still had a lot to learn. But time was passing. I looked at my watch. We had to get moving again. 'I'll go up this time, shall I?'

Alison nodded. 'I'll help you get ready.'

Soon I was back in my seat. I wanted to do another two or three trips to give Thundera as much lightness as possible. She still had four days to go, and I didn't know if the good weather would hold that long.

I was ready to go. 'By the way, Allie,' I asked, 'how did you know she was a female?'

Alison grinned. 'I could see the shape of a young one inside her. Thundera's going to have a baby.'

Soon I was back up in the air. 'Hello Thundera, it's me this time.'

– *Greetings Danny*

'How are you doing? Will you take weight?'

– *I will take weight*

I felt her brush against me and I became lighter. Although it had happened a few times already, suddenly seeing her and feeling the waves still caught me by surprise. And so did the sudden warmth of the air.

'Thank you, Thundera. You can give it back to the rocks. But not yet.'

I enjoyed drifting up to where the waves were stronger. Levity waves. I studied them more carefully. The waves were virtually invisible, with only an occasional glint to show where they were. They were like walls coming towards me, waves of pressure that washed past me, one after the other, endlessly.

Near the beginning of the pool the waves were small and weak, little wavelets that I could hardly feel. But going higher up towards the middle of the pool the waves were bigger and further apart, strong enough to gently rock me as they went past. The strange thing was that they were coming at me from all directions at once, and I was being rocked up and down, side to side and forward and back in a curious figure-of-eight pattern.

*– We are going too far*

Thundera sounded nervous. Nearly 7000 feet again.

'I thought it was better for you higher up, Thundera.'

*– Yes it is, but there is danger*

I looked around. Here and there I could see a few sky-sponges floating in the air, some strands of sky-weed and the occasional flock of sky-fishes. I looked up. It was hard to see the waves and harder to see where the pool ended. Was it miles above me or only a few hundred feet? Some movement caught my eye. Three shapes were diving down towards us. Thundera saw them at the same time.

*– Danger! To the shore!*

The three shapes swooped nearer. I could make them out now. Sharks! Killer sharks, that's what they looked like. The sharks were transparent like the sky-whale, but I could still make out their gaping jaws and rows of vicious teeth. They ignored me and flew straight for Thundera. I saw the one in front strike at Thundera's side as she turned over and beat desperately downwards.

Suddenly I felt something buffet the balloon. The last shark had struck me in passing. Then I heard a sound that made me go cold. The hiss of escaping gas.

## Chapter 11 – A Whale's-eye View

Thundera disappeared below me, chased by the sky-sharks. I had my own problems. The shark had brushed past the balloon, somehow catching the string which went to the escape valve. Gas was hissing out. Already the balloon was starting to sink. It wouldn't be long before I started to drop like a stone.

'Thundera! Are you alright?' I called. A faint reply came from below.

*– Yes, I stay here... alright*

There was a touch of anger too, and the image of a mighty thrashing tail.

*– They would not dare to attack me... if I was free*

The balloon was dropping faster now. The air whistled round my ears and the balloon flapped madly as it fell. I looked down. I was way off Round Hill, but actually that was a good thing. When I hit the earth I would land on soft turf instead of rocky ground. But I was dropping like a lead weight. I didn't know if I would make it this time. I yanked the slipknot to let the rocks go. The balloon slowed down. But I was still going fast. Much too fast. The ground came rushing up to meet me.

I should have been knocked out but I wasn't. I should have broken some bones but I didn't. That's because when I hit the ground I still had some lightness in me. The impact was much softer than normal. I lay thankfully against the earth and after a few moments the missing weight came flooding back into my body.

'Danny!' Alison was running down the slope towards me. 'Danny, are you alright?'

I got stiffly to my feet. 'Yes, I'm okay.' I was just a bit bruised.

'What happened?'

'Some things attacked us. They looked like sharks. Thundera's okay but she had to go lower down to escape from them.'

I looked at Alison. 'Are you okay?' Actually she seemed more shaken than me. Her face was white and she was trembling. I put my arm around her. 'What's the matter?'

'When you were away, Walker came, and the others. They threw your bike off the cliff. It was awful. He was so... I thought he was going to do something to me.'

Walker! Threatening Alison. I burned with anger. 'Where is he!'

She smiled wanly. 'They asked where you were. I told them you'd gone for a five-mile run over the moor. They went away.' Then her face fell again. 'Your bike must be a wreck.'

We walked round to the quarry below the cliff to get my bicycle. It didn't look too bad at first, lying on the rocky floor, but when I got nearer I saw it was a write-off. The frame was broken, the wheels were buckled and the gears were a mangled mess. It had been a good bike, a present from my granddad. I was shattered. It felt like an old friend had died.

Alison invited me to come over to her house after tea.

I found my way to her address and rang the bell. It was a

big house with a well-tended front garden and a BMW in the drive. The door opened and a smartly dressed woman invited me in.

'Hello, you must be Danny, I'm Alison's mother,' she said politely. We shook hands and she ushered me into the well-furnished sitting room. 'Have a seat, Danny.'

I sat down cautiously on the enormous sofa.

'Alison's been telling me all about you,' she went on amiably, just as her daughter came into the room. 'She says you're very good at computers and making things.'

Now it was Alison's turn to be embarrassed. 'Mother! Come on, Danny, I want to show you something in my bedroom.'

She had a large bedroom with an attic style window. I looked round curiously at her posters, furry animals, dresses, and unfamiliar girls' things arranged on her dressing table and around the room.

'Come and look here,' she invited, going to the window. In the bay was a fancy telescope pointing up at the darkening sky. 'I was just getting a fix on Jupiter.'

It was fantastic. I could clearly see the pale striped disk of the planet and four little moons.

She leaned nearer. 'Do you see the moon to the left, the biggest one? That's Ganymede.'

'I'm impressed! What size is the lens?'

'It's not a lens, it's a mirror,' she replied. 'It's six inches. Now I've got a question for you, brain-box. I've given you a clue. How old is Thundera?'

I pulled away from the eyepiece. A clue. Jupiter. 'I know! Thundera said something about the big planet. That must be Jupiter. But I can't remember exactly what she said.'

'Not bad. She said eighty-five turns. Eighty-five orbits.

So what does that make it?'

I was stumped. 'I don't know how long Jupiter's year is. I'd have to look it up.'

Alison was enjoying herself. 'It's 11.86 years. Times eighty-five is one thousand and eight years old!'

I was astonished. I had the impression the sky-whale was only a young adult. They obviously lived a long time. But something puzzled me. 'How would she know about Jupiter?' I asked.

Alison beamed at me. 'They're like astronomers, Danny! The sky-whales know all about the stars and planets. Thundera told me all about it. They're so high up they see the stars just as well as things on the earth below. The stars are more interesting to them. They watch the planets and comets coming and going.'

I could just imagine it. We don't see the stars so well anymore because of all the street lights. But if you go far out into the country on a dark night, the stars seem to hang so close you can almost touch them. Imagine what it must be like miles above the earth.

She went on: 'Thundera can actually see Jupiter's moons. They've got names for them. They can even see other galaxies. She showed them to me in my mind.'

'Those big eyes must be like telescopes,' I ventured.

Alison nodded. 'She's seen such a lot. She told me about her family too. They seem very close. She misses them terribly.'

Her eyes misted. 'And now she's worried about her new baby.'

'Don't worry, she'll be alright,' I said, trying to sound confident. 'We'll do it somehow.'

But we both knew we had problems. Thundera had to stay lower down because of the sharks, which meant she would be gaining more weight. We had to keep taking rocks to her every day until the tide came in. Unfortunately Walker and his gang now knew about the hill, and they were after my blood. Tomorrow was Saturday and I didn't know how I could dodge them over the weekend.

Then we'd have to keep skipping school until Tuesday without being found out. To top it all, I didn't have a bike anymore.

'I'm sorry I can't help you tomorrow,' said Alison. She had to go to a wedding with her parents. 'What are you going to do?'

'I don't know. My mother wants me to help with shopping in the morning. I guess I'll have to carry everything up to the hill in the afternoon. I haven't told my mum about the bike yet.'

But it would be taking a big risk to go out on foot. If Walker's gang found me I wouldn't be able to get away, and they'd wreck the balloon, like they'd trashed my bike. I'd be beaten up, for sure, but I was actually more worried about what they might do to the precious balloon.

If anything happened to it, that would mean the end for the gentle sky-whale and her unborn child.

## Chapter 12 – A New Start

You never know how a day is going to turn out.

I woke up with a feeling of gloom, mainly about my bicycle. I didn't have a definite plan for the day, and the school problem was starting to bother me. My mother and I get on fine, mainly because she trusts me, but she was going to go ballistic when she found out I was playing hooky. I told her about the bike when we were having breakfast.

'I had a bit of an accident yesterday. My bike's really smashed up.'

'Danny! What happened? Are you alright?'

'Yes, I'm okay. The bike went down the hill and hit a rock. The frame's broken and the gears. I don't think it can be fixed.'

'That was from granddad!'

I nodded. I was remembering when he went to the shop with us to get it for my birthday. Just before he died.

Then my mother suddenly brightened up. 'Do you know, Danny, I think he got insurance as well! Let me go and see.'

She came back with the receipt and a hopeful looking document. 'Good old granddad! He thought of everything!'

Sure enough there was an insurance policy covering theft and accidental damage. She read it quickly and passed it to me. 'See! If it's a write-off you can get a new one!'

I couldn't believe my eyes. Granddad was still looking

after me. I felt sad that he was gone. He would have understood about the sky-whale.

Going into the centre that morning was like my birthday all over again. It was just as big a surprise. We went straight to the bicycle store. It's one of my favourite shops. The bikes on display look clean and shiny in their bright colours, and you can smell the newness of their tyres.

The man knew me well. 'Hello Danny, had an accident?'

I was carrying the remains of the bike as evidence. Since he'd sold us the insurance he was able to sort everything out straightaway.

'You can have a new bicycle to the same value, that's what it says. Your luck's in, Danny. I've got some special prices on these mountain bikes this month.'

I couldn't believe it. The ones he showed me were a lot better than the one I had before. Real cross-country bikes with proper shock absorbers; and gears, brakes and everything built for tough conditions.

'Feel the weight,' he said.

I chose one and lifted it up. Very light, considering how strong it looked. And I liked the colour, bright yellow. I looked at my mother. Granddad's gift lived on.

I was dying to try out my new bicycle, but I had to wait until we'd finished the shopping. We put the bike in the back of the car and went on to the supermarket. It was quite busy and we seemed to take ages, but eventually we were finished and ready to go.

'Can you take the trolley to the car, please love?' my mother asked. 'I just want to go to the chemist.' She gave me the car keys and I made my way to the multi-storey car park.

Our car was on the fifth level near the balcony. I'd just raised the back when I heard a voice call out my name.

'Peterson!' It was Walker and, next to him, Tucker.

They raced towards me. I looked round desperately but there was no-one else about. I was alone with two homicidal maniacs. I backed to the balcony wall. The two thugs stood in front of me, blocking my way. Walker didn't lay into me straight away. What he likes to see is fear on his victim's face.

'Got you, you little worm! ' he sneered. Tucker smirked in agreement.

I looked at Walker's face. His ugly mug hadn't been improved by the fall. One eye was half closed, his nose was red and raw and there was a nasty black bruise down the side of his face. He grinned sadistically and lifted his fist. I looked over his shoulder and saw something very interesting.

'Look out!' I said, pointing my finger. 'You're on candid camera!'

Walker spun round and saw what I'd just spotted, a CCTV security camera pointing straight at us.

'That's a police camera,' I said confidently. 'There's a cop looking at you right now. And they record it for evidence.'

Walker looked uncertain. He never did anything in front of witnesses. That's how he'd got away with it for so long.

I pointed to my new shiny yellow bike in the back of the car. 'By the way, Walker, thanks for trashing that old bike of mine. I got a much better one on the insurance. You did me a really big favour.'

Walker scowled. Tucker looked at him, expecting him to reply, but there was nothing the bully could say.

'It's a pity your face wasn't insured,' I went on recklessly. 'You could have got a much better one.'

He stepped towards me. My back was to the wall. For a moment I thought he was going to push me over the balcony, TV camera or not, but he held back. Walker's actually not stupid. He knows what he's doing. Then I said something that *was* stupid. Other people had started to come out to their cars and I was feeling bolder.

'I'm not a push-over like Jason Blant,' I said carelessly.

Walker stared at me with narrowed eyes, wondering how much I knew. He didn't like witnesses. I think that's the moment he decided to do something about me.

## Chapter 13 – The Ghost Walks Again

I decided to ride to the hill before taking out the balloon, to make sure Walker wasn't there.

The new bike was fantastic. The gears could go low enough to ride up the side of a mountain, and the shock absorbers were excellent. As I rode along the stony track I hardly felt the bumps at all. I stopped at the first rise and took out my binoculars. There was no-one to be seen on Round Hill. I scanned the moor around the hill. It looked all clear.

I carried on. When I got near the quarry I stopped and looked around again, checking the path behind me. There was no-one following. But something caught my eye near the cliff. The door of the quarrymen's hut was ajar.

Cautiously I approached the hut, pleased to find that my new cross-country tyres made no sound at all on the bare rock of the quarry floor. Suddenly I caught a whiff of cigarette smoke. Someone was inside the hut. I kept to one side where I couldn't be seen from the window, and stopped again. I listened carefully for a minute, but couldn't hear any voices. Whoever was in there was alone.

Conway was the only one who smoked. Although he's a big hulk he's not very bright and I felt I could deal with him on his own. I put the bike down and crept round the back of the hut until I was near the door. Then I sprang forward, yanked the door shut and slid home the bolt. Conway's startled face appeared at the window. I must say it felt good to have him there as my prisoner this time.

'Hello Conway,' I said pleasantly. 'Having a smoke? I don't smoke myself. Disgusting habit.'

Conway couldn't stop staring at me. 'How did you get out the other day?' he asked.

'That wasn't me. That was my ghost. Ghosts can walk through walls you know.'

Conway gave me a worried look. He's dumb enough to believe anything, if you say it firmly enough.

'You're going to stay here forever, Conway,' I said. 'Your friends are far away and they don't know where you are.'

At that he brightened up. 'That's what you think! They're waiting for you up the hill!'

'Thanks Conway. Just what I wanted to know!'

So Walker and Tucker were planning to ambush me when I got to the top of the hill. I guessed Conway had been given the job of cutting off my retreat. I fetched my bike, wondering what to do next. I could imagine the two bullies hiding up there behind the boulders, waiting for me. But I didn't want to give up and go home. I looked up at the clouds. Somewhere above me Thundera was anxiously waiting for my help.

I decided to go round the foot of the hill, hopefully keeping out of sight of the two thugs above. When I got to the other side of the hill I planned to go further out across the moor, looking for another spot to launch the balloon. I set off, keeping close to the foot of the cliff, and then worked my way round the hill.

I carried on across the moor. The ground was firm and easy to ride on. My new bike was real cool and I was enjoying myself weaving between the clumps of heather. I knew that I'd eventually get to a road that wound back round to the town.

My idea was to return later that way with the balloon and launch it from the moor. As long as it wasn't too far from Round Hill it should be okay, because the sky-whale's pool stretched a couple of miles to each side of the hill. What I was hoping to find was a clump of trees that could keep me hidden while I was getting the balloon ready.

But now the ground was getting soft and wet. My tyres were sinking into the earth. I was riding into a marshy area. I struggled on, keeping to a strip of firmer ground that seemed to go across the marsh. But it was no good. The path petered out in a deep boggy pool. I had to go back and find a way around the marshy section.

I turned the bike round and started back. I could see Round Hill in front of me, the side I didn't normally see. The hill wasn't so steep on this side but sloped gently towards the moor. Suddenly I saw some movement on the hill. Racing towards me down the slope were Walker and Tucker!

They were still some distance away but I knew I must hurry. I had to get back to firm ground again. But it was no good. I was too far out and they were coming too quickly. I was still trapped out on the strip, with soft bog on either side, when they drew up in front of me. I'll never forget the triumphant look on Walker's face.

'Got you, you little rat!'

Tucker sprang forward and dragged me off my bike. I was expecting a beating there and then, but it didn't come.

'Don't touch him!' cried Walker. 'I don't want any marks on him. It's got to look like an accident.'

I was told to pick up my bike and push, and then the two of them marched me back towards the hill. They seemed to have a plan for me all worked out. Walker went in front, I was in the middle pushing my bike, and Tucker followed close behind. I was in a tight spot. I thought desperately for a way out, but I couldn't come up with anything. I didn't even know what they were going to do with me.

Instead of going up the hill they led me back the way I'd come, to the quarry below the cliff. Conway was still locked in the hut. He slunk out sheepishly when the door was opened.

'You let him trick you again,' said Walker icily.

Conway cringed. 'I didn't hear him coming!'

'You were supposed to be looking out for him! Anyway, we've got him now, no thanks to you.'

They bundled me into the hut and hauled my bicycle in too. Walker took out a roll of parcel tape and bound my hands behind my back. He stood back and looked at me with satisfaction.

'You think you're so clever,' he sneered. 'You and that stuck-up tart of yours. Well, you're not. Wait till you see what I've got planned for you.'

'If anything happens to me you'll be in for it,' I said quickly. 'Alison's father's a cop, you know.' And he already had quite a formidable reputation.

Conway looked uncomfortable. Walker glanced at him. 'You go wait outside. See if anyone's coming.'

Walker waited for him to leave the hut before he continued. 'What I've got planned for you is too clever to be found out,' he boasted. 'I've thought of a perfect alibi.'

I stared at him. This sounded ominous.

He grinned sadistically and held up a padlock. 'You're going to stay here while we go back to town. The door will be locked and this time there'll be no Conway to let you out.'

I felt a ray of hope. So they didn't know how I'd done it before. Perhaps I could do it again. But, unfortunately, this time my hands were tied behind my back.

Walker continued. 'Me and Tucker are going ten-pin bowling now. We'll make sure the TV camera gets a good shot of us as we go in. When it gets dark we'll sneak out of a side entrance and come back here.'

He stared at me with hate in his eyes. 'You're going to have an accident, you little smart-ass. They'll say you weren't very smart to go riding on top of the cliff in the dark.'

His voice was gloating now. 'When we've finished with you we'll go back to the bowling alley and come out again through the front entrance. The cameras will show us there all the time. A perfect alibi.'

He got out his roll of tape again and bound a few turns round my ankles. He gave me a shove and I toppled to the floor. Then they left, and I heard the bolt being drawn and the click of the padlock. After a few seconds the sounds of their departure faded away, and I was all alone.

I had to think quickly. It was now five o' clock. Already it was getting hard to see round the hut. The light coming through the tiny window was quite dim. I knew it would be properly dark by six. Walker could be back as early as six-thirty.

I rolled over and struggled to my feet. I looked at my previous escape route. The window was too high up for me now. I couldn't reach it with my hands tied behind my back. Nor could I reach the spanner which I'd hidden on a ledge above the door. I had to get the tape off. But how?

In the movies they use a convenient bit of broken glass to cut through their bonds, but in the hut there was nothing like that. I looked around. Even the old oil lamp was missing its glass cover. I shuffled to the door and pushed on it, pointlessly. Then I realised I was standing on something. It was Conway's lighter.

When you're in danger your brain works overtime. I suddenly knew what to do. I bent down sideways and picked up the lighter with my fingertips. So far so good. Then I shuffled over to the oil lamp. After a bit of a struggle I managed to turn up the wick. A faint smell of paraffin filled the air. I fumbled with the lighter. Click! The wick was lit, but it wouldn't last long.

I burned the sleeves of my jacket, I burned my fingers and I burned my wrists. But I also burned through the parcel tape. Quickly I pulled off the tape round my ankles. I was free! Almost. Once again I unscrewed the bolts and pulled out the grill. I climbed out into the open air and went to the door. Then I realised something. I couldn't get my bike out. The door was padlocked and the window was too small.

I climbed back inside and went over to the door. My luck was in. I could see the screws holding the hinges. I suppose when they fit windows and doors they don't think of people wanting to break in from the wrong side, if you know what I mean.

I took out the screwdriver from my bicycle toolkit. Soon the door was off its hinges and I was able to push it open that way with the padlock still locked. The bike went through next. I looked at the evening sky. Not fully dark yet. There was still enough time to finish off properly.

I went back inside, pulled the door shut and did up the hinges again. The padlock still held the bolt in place. I pocketed the bits of tape and the lighter. It was funny to think that I owed my life to Conway's filthy habit. Then I climbed out through the window and pulled the grill back into place. I was even able to finger-tighten the bolts by reaching my fingers through the grill.

I smiled as I got on my bike. The ghost had walked again.

'You're late, Danny,' said my mum when I went in. 'Are you alright? You look a bit stressed.'

I managed a smile. 'I've been for a ride. The new bike's fantastic.'

I couldn't tell her I'd been kidnapped by Walker and almost pushed off the cliff. Would he really have done it? Had it all just been a cruel bluff? I wasn't sure. They'd seemed deadly serious at the time.

I couldn't tell her I was in danger from the gang whenever I went out on the moor, because I couldn't tell her I kept going up in a balloon. And with someone else's daughter. Nor could I tell her about my narrow escapes up there. My mother would have freaked. Any parent would have freaked. Not only was it hair-raisingly dangerous, it was also illegal to fly a balloon like that without a licence.

So I said nothing and just ate my supper.

After supper I had a hot bath and thought about what to do next. The day had passed without us helping the sky-whale, and Sunday wasn't going to be any good either. But there *was* something we could do. I wished Alison was home so I could talk to her about it.

It was quite late when she phoned me. 'How did it go today?' she asked cheerfully.

'Not very good. I got caught by Walker but I got away.'

'Are you alright?'

'Yeah I'm okay.' I didn't go into details just then, though

I did later.

'I haven't been able to go up at all.'

'Oh no! What about Thundera? She must be wondering where you are.'

'I know. Tomorrow's not going to be easy either. But I've got an idea.'

'What, Danny?'

I took a deep breath. 'Allie, I want to go up tonight.'

## Chapter 14 – Flying Blind

The sky-whale was relying on us to help her. The only thing I could do was to go up in the balloon that night.

'I'm coming with you!' said Alison.

I didn't argue with her this time. I was glad to have her with me. 'Can you get away alright?' I asked.

'I think so. I'll go to bed now and then climb out the window. I've got a rope in my room my father gave me for a fire escape. I've tried it before. Where shall we meet?'

'At my place. Come through the garden and go straight to the shed. Don't turn the light on. I'll meet you there once my mum goes to bed. Bring a torch.'

Luckily I didn't have to wait very long. Five minutes later my mother popped her head into my room.

'Goodnight, Danny,' she said. 'Don't stay up too late.'

'Goodnight Mum.' I waited a few minutes, turned off my light, then crept downstairs.

It was pitch black outside. Alison was just coming through the garden and we bumped into each other in the darkness.

'Hello Danny,' she whispered.

I guided her to the shed and switched on my torch.

'You've got a new bike!'

'Thanks to my granddad,' I grinned. 'The old one was insured.'

Alison seemed as pleased as I was. 'You're very lucky,

Danny!'

We loaded on the balloon, gas cylinder, ropes, bags and all the other equipment, and I added a spare torch. Finally we were ready to go. Alison passed me my coat and helped me on with it.

'Okay?' she whispered. I nodded and smiled back at her. It felt like we were running away together.

It was pitch black on the moor. There was no moon and the stars were hidden by cloud. We weren't riding since Alison hadn't been able to bring her bike, but I don't think we could have ridden anyway. The track was in total darkness. Once we got over the first rise it felt like we were really out in the wilds. The lights of the town dipped out of sight behind us and everything was quiet, apart from the call of an owl. I felt a few drops of rain on my face and Alison drew closer to me.

I knew there would be no danger from Walker at this time of night. They would have cleared off as soon as they saw I was gone. When we reached the quarry I led Alison to the hut and checked the door. The padlock was no longer there.

'I think I should tell my dad about him,' said Alison seriously.

'But your father might ask about him at school, and find out we've been absent.'

'Mm. You're right. He knows Mr Grayson quite well, they're on a committee together.'

Anyway, the police couldn't do very much. There weren't any witnesses to what had happened. It would be my word against Walker's, and that wasn't good enough.

Once we reached the hilltop we made our base in the hollow between the boulders, and got the equipment ready by the light of Alison's torch. The night was black. Looking up I could see a few stars coming and going, showing that clouds must be moving across the sky, but I couldn't tell how fast they were travelling.

'Are you sure it's okay to go, Danny?' asked Alison nervously. The balloon was tugging to one side in the breeze and we knew that the cliff edge, invisible in the darkness, was not far away.

I shrugged. It was going to be really scary just going up into the blackness, never mind being blown off course. But we had to try.

'I'll be okay. Give me twenty minutes then start shining the torch up,' I said. 'I'll try to get back here, but I might have to come down off the hill. Don't come running in the dark.'

'Okay.' But she still seemed reluctant to let go the rope.

Suddenly she leaned towards me. 'Good luck, Danny.' I felt a quick kiss on my cheek. Then she loosened her grip on the rope, and the balloon pulled me up and away. I could see the waving of her torch as I rose, and I waved back with mine. I could tell by the way her light moved to one side that I was being carried away by the wind. I was going in the direction of the town, but I was also rising quite fast. I reckoned I should still reach the sky-pool alright.

The next problem was the sky-whale. Would she be able to see me?

I waved my torch around. 'Hello Thundera. I'm here!'

*– Greetings Danny... I am tired... come...*

I waved the torch some more. 'Can you see me?'

*– Come further... quickly please*

'I'm coming. Hang on!'

As I rose I could see the lights of the town quite clearly on one side, like a shiny island in a black sea, drifting ever

closer. Suddenly the lights vanished completely. For a few
seconds a white mist swirled in the light of my torch. Then I
could see the stars, millions of them, shining brightly in the
jet black sky above.

> – *Greetings... I see you now... you are close... will
> you take weight?*

'Yes. But first push me back...' But it was too late. I felt
the balloon lurch as the rocks doubled in weight.

> – *Thank you ... you are good...*

'Quickly, can you push me back to the hill! The middle
of the pool!'

I felt a nudge and then we were moving, surging through
the sky. But not fast enough. I could see the cloud tops,
shining palely in the starlight, coming up to meet me.

> – *Farewell... come again... please*

The sky-whale had to leave me. How far had we gone? I
wouldn't know till I dropped through the clouds. For a
while all I could see was blackness then at last a tiny light
flashed up towards me. But I wasn't going to come down
anywhere near Round Hill. The wind was blowing me back
towards town. I could see the lights of the houses. Then the
lights suddenly disappeared below the horizon and I braced
myself. The sack hit the ground and the balloon slowed to a
stop.

Far away across the moor I could see Alison's light
winking at me from the top of the hill and I flashed back at
her. Then the balloon lurched as the rocks shed their
weight, and once again I started to rise.

This time I made sure Thundera pushed me well past the
hill before she gave weight.

'Are we over the hill?' I couldn't see Alison's light while I
was above the clouds.

*– Now we are there*

'Good. Now push me even further, please.'

After a couple of minutes I guessed we'd gone far enough.

'Okay, now give weight!'

*– I give weight... thank you*

This time my position was much better than before, and when I slid down through the clouds I spotted Alison's torch straightway. Quickly I flashed back. The wind blew me steadily towards the light and as I got nearer I was so close I thought I was going to land right on top of her. But at the last moment I sailed over her head. The sack of rocks missed her by inches. Then I was over the edge of the cliff and dropping towards the quarry floor. Not bad aim, considering. In fact, nearly perfect.

I made three more flights up into the blackness, and three more blind descents. By that time Thundera must have dumped a couple of hundred pounds. I wondered what she'd weigh if she didn't have any lightness. Thousands of pounds, probably.

'Are you alright, now?' I asked her. I was tired and shivering with cold.

> *– I have good lightness but... the pool is lowering with the new tide... I must stay lower because of the sharks ... and deathly heaviness will afflict me... keep coming... three more days... please Danny...*

'Okay, I'll try. I'm going back to shore now.'

Soon we were back in position. The clouds had broken up as the hours had gone by, and now I could actually see Alison's light winking far below.

'Goodbye Thundera.'

*– Farewell little one...*

Down I went. I kept my torch flashing in Alison's direction all the way. By sheer good luck I touched down on the hilltop not too far away and she was able to run and grab the mooring rope. I didn't let the gas out straightaway, but let Alison pull on the rope till I was almost touching the ground. It was very late, two in the morning, but I still thought I might go up again while we had the chance.

'How are you? How's Thundera?' she asked anxiously.

'I'm freezing! She seemed desperate but she's okay now. We have to keep going. Three more days, she says.'

'Are you staying down now?'

I wanted to stop, but I wasn't sure.

'I don't know. The more weight she can lose the better.'

'You look shattered, Danny. I'll go up.'

I looked at her. The wind was getting quite strong. The last couple of times Thundera had needed to push me all the way to the side of the pool, about two miles into the moor. The situation was getting worse. I shouldn't really have let Alison go, but I did.

'Okay.' I undid my straps, and slid down the rope to the ground. Then I held the balloon down until she had strapped herself safely into the seat.

'You must tell Thundera to push you across the moor. Like she did for me. She'll know what to do.'

'Okay.' The night was black, the air was cold and the balloon was flapping in the wind, but Alison looked happy enough.

I let go of the rope and waved her on her way.

It always seemed more scary to watch Alison going up than to go up myself. She looked so precarious dangling below the balloon. Soon all I could see was her torch light winking upwards. Then it seemed to disappear.

A cold wind was blowing across the hilltop. I shivered, and huddled down to wait in the shelter of the hollow between the boulders. I thought about the strange adventure we were having. A week ago I hadn't even tried out my new balloon, and Alison Day was just a girl I sometimes chatted to.

Since then I'd been up countless times, had met a fantastic creature, and felt the mysterious force of the waves in the sky. And Alison and I had suddenly become real friends, sharing in the most amazing adventure of our lives.

High up across the moor a light twinkled in the blackness like a star. Like a shooting star. Alison was being pushed across the sky. Then she started to come down. I watched the light drifting downwards. But she was moving too fast sideways. The wind was too strong. She wasn't going to land on the hill. She passed high over my head and kept on going. Eventually I saw the light reach ground level, some distance away, halfway to the village.

'Dump the gas!' I yelled, but the wind blew my words away. I knew what was going to happen. If she took off from there again, with the wind this strong, she would miss the sky-pool. Thundera wouldn't be able to reach her to give her weight, or to push her back towards me.

The balloon would rise up, and keep rising, and she would be blown away high over the town. Alison had to let out the gas while she was still safely on the ground. But did she realise that?

## Chapter 15 – Rough Justice

I jumped on my bike and rode as fast as I dared down the path, lighting my way with the torch. Alison was about to go sailing away through the night sky and I had to stop her. But even as I started down the hillside I saw her twinkling light rising up again.

I raced along the track in the darkness, trying to keep my eyes on her light. Would she make it to Thundera's sky-pool this time? I should've been looking where I was going. Crash! I ploughed into a bank on a bend. I picked myself up and carried on more carefully.

When I got to the last rise and saw the lights of the town I stopped to take a bearing. Alison was quite high, and still rising, and I knew she must have missed the sky-pool. She was just crossing from moor to village; my house was probably straight below her.

If she did nothing she would rise higher and higher in the freezing air, and drift right across the country. She would have to let out some gas to come down. I guessed she'd wait till she was past all the lights of the town before doing that. There was nothing I could do except follow her. I carefully checked the direction she was going and tried to figure out where she would end up. Then I headed into the town.

The balloon was impossible to see through the glare of the street-lamps, and for a while I lost her. I pedalled furiously through the deserted streets, trying to keep to the direction I'd last seen her light moving.

It would be dangerous coming down in the dark. On the other side of the town there were all sorts of hazards. First there was a strip of woodland, and further out a row of electric pylons, all hidden in the darkness. Alison was new to the area. Would she know they were there? If it was me I would try to come down in the ploughed land just after the trees. I followed the road out of town and after a while I stopped to search the sky. At last I spotted her. High up, but starting to descend, was a small twinkling light.

My road dipped down a hill, crossed a stream, ran through the woods. It was a difficult ride in the darkness since I was steering with one hand and holding my torch in the other. But it was nothing compared to what Alison was doing. She was coming down blind in unknown territory. She could easily crash into the treetops or, worse still, fly right into the high voltage cables.

I got through the woods and reached the farmer's fields. I stopped and clambered up a bank to peer over the hedge. Some distance away, at ground level, was the welcome sight of a waving torch. I ran to meet her.

Alison had landed safely in the middle of the field. She was on a high after her unexpected jaunt over the town.

'Hello Danny, were you worried?' she laughed, as I helped her down from her seat.

'Yes I was. I'm glad you missed the pylons!'

'What pylons?' she asked blankly.

I turned my beam to the end of the field. A row of gaunt skeletons loomed up out of the darkness, between them stretched humming wires. 'Those ones!'

We both slept late that Sunday morning. When I finally got

up I was feeling optimistic about the sky-whale. I thought we could go out again late afternoon when no-one else was about.

Alison thought that would be good idea too. 'Come over to my house for supper,' she suggested when I phoned her. 'Then I'll say I'm going back with you for the evening. I should be okay till nine-thirty.'

In the afternoon I spent a couple of hours going over the equipment and cleaning my new bike, then I changed and got ready to go. It felt a bit like I was like going on a date.

'You do look smart, Danny,' said my mum as I was leaving. 'Give my love to Alison. Have a good time!'

Alison's mother opened the door to me again.

'Hello Danny. Come in,' she said politely.

I'd passed a patrol car in the drive when I'd come through, parked behind the BMW, and I could hear voices in the study, Alison's father and a work colleague. I felt a bit nervous. I'd yet to meet Inspector Day. When he finally finished his business and joined us for tea he had some interesting news.

'There've been some reports of lights in the sky,' he told us, 'over the moor. Do you believe in UFO's, Danny?'

I nearly choked on my pizza. 'Um, I don't know,' I said weakly and Alison giggled. Inspector Day stared at me as though I was a reluctant suspect who wouldn't spill the beans.

I blushed. 'I mean, yeah, probably.'

He stared even harder at me. 'Tell me, Danny, what are you going to do when you finish school?'

I hadn't been expecting Alison's father to give me the third degree.

'Um, computing,' I managed.

'What sports do you play?'

Alison was looking uncomfortable. 'Dad, can you pass the salad please,' she said quickly.

Just then the phone rang. Inspector Day sighed and got up from the table. 'Excuse me, that'll be the station again.'

But it wasn't. When he returned to the dining room Alison and I could see that something was wrong. Very wrong. He didn't sit down again.

'That was Mr Grayson,' he said in an icy voice. 'He spotted you in town on Friday, Alison. He said you two haven't been to school for the past three days.'

Alison went pale. Mrs Day gasped. Then the inspector turned to me. His face was going red and I thought he was going to yank me from my seat.

'Get out, Peterson. I don't want your sort here. Get out, stay away from my daughter and don't come back!'

## Chapter 16 – No Going Back

When I got home my mother was waiting for me. Inspector Day had obviously called her. She looked upset. She was almost in tears.

'I'm shocked, Danny. I thought I could trust you. What on earth have you been doing?'

I looked down, not knowing what to say.

'Mr Day was very rude to me. He said you were a bad influence.'

I still didn't know what to say.

'But I wasn't having that,' she went on, with a toss of her head. 'I said if anyone's the bad influence it must be that Alison. You never played truant before you met her.'

She looked directly at me. 'What have you two been doing, Danny?'

'We've just been going out together on our bikes.'

'But why did you have to stay away from school?'

My mother was honestly baffled, and I couldn't give her any real explanation. I imagined Alison being asked the same questions and giving the same non-answers.

'We just did.'

She sighed. 'Well anyway, you're to report to Mr Grayson first thing tomorrow morning. I'll drop you off at school. He'll have something to say to you.'

'Okay.'

She frowned unhappily. 'I'm grounding you, Danny. I'm

afraid it's no more bicycle and no more seeing Alison Day.'

I had to lock my bike in the shed and give her the key.

Putting on my school clothes the next morning was an awful letdown. School clothes meant a return to a life dull and ordinary. And they also meant letting down our mysterious and gentle friend, up in the sky.

'Are you ready to go?' My mother was still cross with me.

When we got to school I had to walk with her to the office like a little kid. She was quite embarrassed to speak to the secretary.

'Er, I believe Mr Grayson wants to see Danny first thing,' she said.

'Oh? He'd better wait in here,' said the secretary.

'I'll be off then.' My mother was still waiting for me to say sorry but somehow I couldn't.

'Okay. Bye Mum.'

I sat down. We'd come early and I had some time to wait. Other kids stared at me curiously as they went past the window hatch on their way in. Just before the bell rang Alison and her mother appeared. Mrs Day glanced disdainfully at me through the hatch.

'My daughter has an appointment with Mr Grayson at nine,' she announced. 'My husband spoke with him at the weekend.'

'Another one. Come in here then, Alison, and wait. He shouldn't be long.'

Kids were surging past now. School was starting. We waited a few more minutes. Alison and I hadn't spoken though we'd exchanged secret smiles. She was pale, but she still looked determined. More time passed. The Monday morning hubbub died down as everyone settled into their classes, called registers, started lessons.

'I don't know where Mr Grayson is,' said the secretary. 'Perhaps you should go to class.'

Just then the phone rang. The secretary answered it.

'That was him,' she told us. 'He's going to be away this morning. He wants to see both of you at lunchtime.'

We got up and went out into the corridor. Alison looked at me. We could turn left and go on into the school. Or we could turn right and walk out through the front door. The secretary's back was turned. We hurried out of the school.

It felt as though eyes were boring into my back as we walked down the steps and along the driveway. I expected someone to challenge us every step of the way. Some children and even teachers must have seen us through their classroom windows, but I suppose they had other things to get on with. Ten more steps to the school gates, then we would be safely out of sight behind the fence. I held my breath. At last we were through the gates and round the corner. We'd done it!

'Just keep walking naturally,' said Alison.

She took a file out of her bag, folded it back and walked as though she was making notes. We could have been a pair of students doing a geography survey. I was grinning with relief, although we were not yet in the clear. We still had some way to walk, past shops and houses, before we'd get home.

'I'm sorry my father spoke to you like that yesterday,' said Alison. 'That wasn't fair.'

'It's okay.'

'He doesn't know you like I do, Danny. You're brave and caring and you know how to get things done. Not many boys would have the guts to do what you do.'

You're not bad either, I thought, but I didn't know how to say it.

'Was your mum cross?' she went on.

'Yeah, she was pretty upset.'

'I'm sorry. I like her. My parents were furious. They couldn't believe it.'

What we were doing now was even more unbelievable. Open defiance of parents *and* headmaster. I hadn't thought much beyond the act of getting away, but now we had to make our plans very carefully.

'We'll need to stay out of sight for two days,' I said.

The implications were awesome. We would be run-aways. My mother would be pretty worried and I could imagine the fuss Alison's father would make. He would launch a manhunt for us.

There was no time to waste. With luck our absence wouldn't be noticed at first, but when we didn't show up at lunchtime Mr Grayson would start to investigate. And it wouldn't be long before he called Inspector Day.

When we got home the first thing I did was look for the key to the shed. I had an idea where it might be. I went into my mother's room and looked on the top shelf of her wardrobe. That's where she used to put things she'd taken from me when I was little. Sure enough there was the key.

'Sorry, Mum,' I whispered.

The next thing we did was change out of our school clothes. Alison chose a pair of my jeans, sweatshirt and jumper for herself. I must say she looked real cool in them. She hung up her dress and cardigan neatly in my wardrobe.

Then we went to the shed. I dug out the camping gear we used to use with granddad and spread it out on the floor. There would be a lot to carry. We selected two sleeping bags, a small tent, some cooking things and water bottles.

'What are we going to do for food?' asked Alison.

We went back inside and had a look. There was nothing much in the fridge.

'Let me go back to that shop on the corner,' said Alison. 'I'll get some bread and things for sandwiches.'

I went and got some money for her. 'Be careful,' I said. I didn't want any last-minute hitches. But I was being over-cautious. The only real danger would be seeing someone who knew her father, such as a passing policeman. I carried on packing the balloon and other equipment. It was quite a load since I had to take an extra gas cylinder this time.

Finally all the gear was ready and so was the food. Alison raided the bathroom for soap and stuff while I took the final step. A note for our parents.

I addressed it to my mother: *Dear Mum, Alison and I are going away for a couple of days. We will be back soon. Do not worry. Love Danny.*

We tidied the shed and I locked it and replaced the key. My mother would probably still look to see if my bike was gone, but she wouldn't notice the camping things were missing unless she rummaged through everything. I locked up the house.

'Ready Danny?' Alison was carrying a heavy rucksack.

I took hold of my fully-laden bicycle. 'Yes. Let's go!'

## Chapter 17 – Going Camping

Maybe it's being a policeman's daughter that makes Alison so fearless. She was in high spirits as we walked up the track, humming to herself as she strode along. We could've been going on a picnic. I was the nervous one, expecting cops to come running after us at any moment. Alison had no such worries. She turned her head and smiled at me.

'You look nice in my clothes,' I ventured.

'Thank you. Nicer than you'd look in mine!' She giggled at the thought.

'You never expected all this, did you Allie? Are you glad you moved here?'

'I wasn't at first. But I am now.' She smiled. ' I never expected to meet someone as crazy as you, Danny.'

'Thanks! I'm also glad you came to live here.'

She gave me another smile.

After a while we changed over and I carried the rucksack while she pushed the bike. We decided to go up Round Hill first, although we wouldn't be staying there. There was a light breeze on the hilltop, blowing the same direction as before, towards the town. Scattered clouds drifted in the sky, though there was no sign of rain.

I concentrated. 'Thundera!' I called. 'Can you hear me?'

Alison joined in. 'Thundera!'

We waited and listened. Then I heard a very faint whisper in my head.

*– I am here... come soon... please*

'Were coming, hold on!' cried Alison.

But we still had further to go. They would come looking for us on Round Hill, and there was also the problem of Walker and his gang. We walked to the far side of the hilltop. Down below was the moor I'd tried to cross the time Walker caught me. From up on the summit it was easy to see the watery area. Now I could see where I should've gone, around the marsh to the left.

'Can you give me the binoculars please,' I asked.

Alison got them out of the rucksack. 'Here you are.'

We needed a base. I scanned the countryside and saw mostly grass and heather. But one spot looked promising, a clump of greenery a mile or two further on.

'See there,' I said, handing over the binoculars. 'It looks like some trees.'

'Looks good. Shall we go for them?'

We set off down the slope and through the heather in the direction of the distant trees, skirting the marshland. It seemed further on the ground and we struggled a bit over the rough terrain. But then we found an animal trail, a faint path that wandered in the direction we wanted to go, so we followed that.

'The heather's gorgeous, isn't it,' said Alison. There were two kinds in bloom, a deep purple heath and also a paler lilac one. Bees worked busily to get in their last harvest of the year. I breathed deeply. It was good being out in the wilds and having it all to ourselves.

The little copse we'd chosen was just right. We pushed through a thicket of bushes and stopped beneath the sheltering trees. Alison and I looked at each other. It couldn't have been more perfect. A dozen trees close together with a space in between for our camp. We dumped our stuff and had a quick look round. There were soft, sweet-smelling pine needles on the ground, and nearby a stream trickled into a crystal-clear pool with mossy banks. This was definitely where we would spend the night.

Meanwhile we had more urgent things to do. We carried the balloon out into the open and began getting everything ready.

'Do you think we're still underneath the sky-pool?' asked Alison.

'I think we're just on the edge of it. But the breeze will take us towards the middle.'

'You go first, Danny,' said Alison generously. I knew she was dying to go up. We both were.

Soon I was on my way. I checked to see how much I was drifting. By the time I reached the clouds I was about half-way to Round Hill. 'Hello Thundera, I'm coming!'

    *– Greetings... I am very thankful... to see you*

She met me at 4500 feet. The pool had lowered quite a bit.

    *– I am here*

'Push me that way, then give weight.'

I felt her nudge me, then we were moving back the way I'd come. She seemed to be swimming more slowly this morning.

'How are you today?'

    *– I am well... but heaviness assails me... the waves*
      *feel weak*

'Don't worry, we're here now. We'll keep coming to help you.'

    *– You are faithful... the pool is growing bigger...*
      *soon I will be free... with my family... thanks to*
      *you... and your mate...*

'Where are the sharks?'

I got an angry image of a tail slamming into a shark and sending it spinning away.

> – *They are about... and now my new one... makes it harder for me*

'Do you mean your new young one?'

> – *Yes... the new one will soon swim*

'That's good.'

> – *I can go no further*

'That'll be okay. Now give weight.'

> – *I give weight... thank you*

'Bye, I'll be back.'

She had pushed me over the moor almost to our camp, but the breeze wafted me away from it. The sack splashed down in the bog. I was glad I was hanging up in the air. Then the extra weight drained out of the rocks and I was off again.

It was better being on this side of the hill far away from the village and prying eyes, and I was enjoying the different view for a change. As I rose I could see more of the open moor and only a little of the town in the distance. It was turning into a fine day.

I went up and down a couple of times. The breeze began to die down, and each time I landed I was a bit closer to our camp site. Finally I came down on the firmer ground close to the trees. Alison came running out to grab the mooring rope.

'Can I have a turn now?' she called.

'Yeah, pull me down.'

'How is she?'

'She's fine now. She said her calf is due soon.'

'Ooh Danny!'

She eagerly hauled me down and took my place.

'Bye Danny, see you around!'

I smiled and waved her on her way.


Alison had been busy while I was away. She'd put the tent up and when I looked inside I saw that she'd gathered a thick bed of pine needles for us to lie on. The two sleeping bags were neatly laid out side by side. She'd also left out a pack of sandwiches for me, and an apple. I was starving.

I thought about school as I ate my lunch. Just about now Mr Grayson would be doing his nut at our absence. No-one ever defied him. No-one would dare. What would Grayson do next? Phone Inspector Day, I should think. And I knew what he was like.

Would they start looking for us straightaway? If they phoned my mother she might go home at lunchtime and see my note, and think we'd run away. Then Alison's father would really blow his top. That didn't matter, nothing mattered, as long as we could stay hidden on the moor for another day.

I fetched the binoculars and focused on Round Hill, staying in the shadow of the bushes. Even now a policeman could be up there with binoculars of his own, looking my way.

Then I searched for the silver dot above me. Up among the clouds the balloon was hard to see unless you were actually looking for it. The risky time was when it was going up or down. Then it was easier to spot.

Alison was coming down now. The breeze had stopped and she was dropping vertically a little way out from me. She seemed to be falling slowly, and I guessed Thundera had given her extra lightness. I ran across with the binoculars and I tossed them up to her.

'Catch! Go over Round Hill next time and see if anyone's there!'

'Okay!'

'Thanks for the lunch!'

She waved a ghostly hand and the balloon lifted up. I found a soft spot in the heather and lay down to watch as the silver sphere shrank to a dot, and smiled when it started to move mysteriously across the sky. No wonder people were talking about UFO's. The balloon hovered high above Round Hill for a time, then moved behind a cloud. The light was bright and I closed my eyes to rest them. Before I knew it I'd drifted off to sleep.

I woke with a start. Someone was calling my name.

'Danny, where are you!'

I jumped up. The balloon was on the ground and just starting to rise up again. I ran forward and grabbed the rope just in time.

'Danny, there was a police car there! What should I do?'

'Where was it?'

'On the quarry road. I could see two policemen walking round the top of the hill.'

'Are they still there?'

'No. We hid in a cloud till they left. That's why I was so long. Should I go up again?'

'What do you think?'

'Up there I can see if anyone's around before I come down. I think it's okay.'

'Alright.' The sky-whale needed all the lightness we could give her. We were nearly there. I felt a thrill of excitement. Tomorrow would be Thundera's big day.

Alison carried on until late afternoon. Finally she came

down for the last time and let out the gas. The balloon collapsed on the heather with a sigh, and so did Alison, still dizzy from lightness. I went to help her. Suddenly I heard a deep drumming noise, growing ever louder. We looked at each other in puzzlement. Then it sank in.

'Helicopter!' I yelled. Alison jumped up. The silvery fabric of the balloon was spread out like a signal sheet. They couldn't miss it.

# Chapter 18 – A Night Out

'Untie the bags!' I yelled.

I ran round the balloon, stretched out on the ground. Fold, fold, fold. That would have to do. I bundled the silky fabric up in my arms.

'Leave the sack. Run!'

We ran for our lives without looking back. There was no time. The sound grew louder. We got under the trees just as the helicopter came over a rise. We crouched down with pounding hearts. Had they seen us? The machine clattered overhead without slowing, and just as quickly the sound faded away. We hadn't even been able to see what kind of helicopter it was, it had all happened so quickly. We looked at each other. Had we got away with it?

'It probably wasn't even looking for us,' said Alison.

I wasn't so sure.

'Do you think it's okay to make a fire?' asked Alison.

The evening was cool, and we needed the warmth. We also wanted a hot meal, but we didn't want our campfire to be spotted.

'It'll be okay right in the trees,' I replied.

We arranged some boulders for a fireplace and gathered up dry branches. Soon we had a crackling fire going. I put on a couple of bigger logs and the fire settled down to a steady burn. Alison put on a pan of water and when it boiled she added a packet of noodles. The warm spicy aroma blended nicely with the smell of burning pine wood.

'There you go, Danny.'

'Thanks!'

'You're the first boy I've cooked for.'

'I'm impressed. Your instant noodles are fantastic. Now I'll show you what I can do.'

I took two cheese sandwiches and leaned them against one of the hot rocks close to the embers. When one side was nicely toasted I turned them over and did the other side.

I handed one to Alison, hot and oozing with melted cheese. 'There you go!'

'Thank you, genius. So you're not just a pretty face.'

'You're the first girl I've spent the night with.'

'Don't get ideas, Peterson!'

'They'll think we've run away together.'

'Me, run away with you! I don't think so.' But her eyes sparkled.

After our meal we made some tea and settled down together to watch the flickering yellow flames. The fire burned down and I put another log on. We didn't want to go to bed. It grew colder and we snuggled up. I was lost in thought and so was Alison. We were both thinking about the past days and what the morning would bring. Alison was the first to break our pensive silence.

'Thundera was different today. She was showing me how to give weight like I was her calf. It must be some kind of instinct.'

'Yeah, she wanted me to do it too, the other day,' I replied.

'I got really light, like I was floating. It was fantastic. I could feel the waves, and see her so clearly...' Her voice trembled. 'But after tomorrow we'll never see her again.'

I tried to comfort her. 'You don't know. She might come back next year.'

'No, they usually stay high up in their ocean,' she went on. 'It's actually too dangerous lower down in the pool. She won't risk it again. And the big ocean's too high for us to reach in the balloon.'

I didn't know what to say. She was right. 'And we'll never feel the waves or see those other sky-creatures again,' she went on dolefully.

I held her hand. 'At least we *have* seen it. No-one else has.' I tried to sound positive but I wasn't fooling anyone.

She pressed closer to me. 'And her baby. It's due any day. I wish I could've seen it.'

I put my arm around her. 'I know.'

I woke up in the dark. For a moment I didn't know where I was.

'Danny, come and look!' Alison was at the tent flap, calling me out.

I wriggled out of my sleeping bag. 'What is it?'

She led me through the bushes onto the open moor. The heather glowed mistily in the pre-dawn light. Not a thing stirred.

'Look!'

High over Round Hill, alone in the eastern sky, rose a thin silver crescent. Today was the day. The new moon had arrived.

## Chapter 19 – The Time Comes

I made a fire with some twigs and pine-needles and heated water for tea, while Alison washed her face in the pool. There were still some sandwiches left and I carried them out with our drinks. Sunrise was starting. We sat down on the heather to have our breakfast and watched the top of Round Hill turn a rosy pink.

'Do you know why the pool is over Round Hill?' asked Alison suddenly.

I shook my head.

'It's a lens! Don't you see. It focuses the levity waves!'

I pictured the huge ball of granite hidden beneath the softer earth. An enormous lens focusing strange forces, the way a magnifying glass focuses the sun's rays into a cone of light, shifting and changing as it moves around.

'Yeah. Could be. But where do they come from?'

'I don't know. Have you heard of gravity waves? Maybe the waves from the earth and the moon interfere with each other and cause levity waves. And the pattern would keep changing.'

I nodded. It seemed a good theory.

'There are probably other Round Hills and other pools! We should ask her...' She broke off and her eyes went moist. There would be little more chance to talk to the sky-whale. Thundera was leaving today.

I got up. 'Come on, let's get going.'

'Are you okay?' I asked, as we started to carry the gear out into the open.

'Yes I'm fine now.' She smiled bravely. 'She's going to see her family soon. Think how happy she must be.'

By a miracle we'd made it to the final day. I thought of all the obstacles we had faced and overcome. Nothing more could go wrong now. Or could it?

'Oh no! Feel the wind!' cried Alison. The early morning stillness had given way to a breeze blowing towards us from the hill.

'We can't launch from here,' I agreed. 'We'll be blown the wrong way. We must get nearer the hill.'

I began loading the bike while Alison emptied the rocks out of the sack. It was too heavy to carry like that.

'Let's just go, and leave the other stuff here,' she said.

I agreed. The tent could wait. It was more important to get the balloon safely up in the air, before anyone found us. We pushed our way through the heather until we were half-way to the hill.

'This should be okay,' I said.

Alison looked around. 'There are no stones here,' she said anxiously.

She was right. We needed plenty of rocks but there were none to be seen in the peaty earth. We had to go on. Eventually we reached the base of the hill. I started filling the balloon while Alison gathered up stones. It all seemed to be taking a long time. I kept glancing up the hillside, half expecting to see someone there, looking down on us. But finally everything was ready.

'I just want to make one last trip to say goodbye,' said Alison, looking me in the eyes. 'But you can be the one to see her off, Danny. You're the one who made it all happen.'

I got a bit choked. 'Thanks, Alison,' I managed.

She smiled and climbed into the seat.

'Try to land on the hill,' I called. 'I'll go up there now. But if anyone comes, don't worry about me. Just keep going up and down yourself.'

She nodded, and I let go the rope.

I pushed the bike up the hill feeling very relieved. No-one could interfere now. Nothing more could go wrong. Soon the levity waves would make a channel to the ocean in the sky, and Thundera would have enough lightness to swim through, back to her family and the safety of the deep.

I laid my bike in the hollow between the boulders, and walked over to the cliff edge to survey the scene below. There was no sign of anyone near the quarry or on the track. No police vehicles. I went back to wait. After a while I saw the balloon coming down towards me. Alison landed nearby and I ran to grab the rope. She slid down next to me with a happy smile on her face.

'How is she?'

'She's fine. She's very keen to go. The channel's not open yet but it will be soon.'

'And you said goodbye?'

She nodded. 'Thundera was great. She's happy now. She said some nice things.'

I took her place in the seat and we looked at each other again. It was a big moment. 'See you, Allie.'

'See you, Danny.'

The balloon lifted and Round Hill dropped away. I wouldn't be seeing that sight so often, after the sky-whale went away. The hill grew smaller and the air grew colder.

   – *Greetings Danny... I am here*

I could sense her invisible presence. 'Hello Thundera. Your day has come. You must be pleased.'

*– I am very happy...*

'What do you want to do? How much more lightness do you need?'

I picked up a feeling. It was the urge to get moving, a desperate longing to ride the big ocean waves, to be with others of her kind, to have their protection for something that was about to happen.

> *– I must go up... I feel the changing waves... it is nearly time... but I need more lightness... come twice more... that will be enough*

'Okay. But first will you take weight from me? Not too much. Give it back to the rocks.'

Once again the beautiful creature appeared before my eyes, the air turned warm and I felt the waves. She pushed me past the hill, gave weight to the rocks, and set me on my downwards course. Twice more I went down, then up for the very last time.

'Will this be enough for you?'

> *– Yes, it is enough... I will be able to go through... when the channel opens...*

'Are you going now?'

> *– I wish to go up... though I must still wait... some little time...*

I was still rising, waiting for her to give weight to the rocks. Thundera was rising up with me.

> *– You should have more lightness... little Danny...*

I sensed a curious motherly feeling coming from the great sea-whale, like I was her calf or something. And I had a strange feeling myself; a need to have more lightness, to be just the same as my big companion.

'Can you spare the lightness?' I asked.

> *– I have enough for you, little one... come... you try again this time ...*

She nudged against me, and I tried to remember how to do it.

*– No, like this... first I give... then you push...*

I pushed and suddenly I felt my weight draining away, lots of it. A satisfying feeling of getting rid of something, of passing into a dreamy state, of seeing things differently. Thundera looked quite solid now, a rosy grey colour. Things floated or swam around us that I hadn't noticed before. The waves were still virtually invisible, but I could feel them strongly now, rhythmic surges washing against me and somehow through me. It was hard to think. The balloon was shooting up.

'Give weight to the rocks,' I cried.

Thundera brushed against the sack. The balloon slowed. Then she said something mind-bogglingly crazy.

*– Let go of your bubble, Danny... I will give you*
*more lightness... swim free little one... do not*
*worry... when I depart you can drift down to the*
*shore... safely*

I must have been drunk from the lightness. It actually seemed like a good idea. I pulled the valve open and tied the string. Gas hissed out. Then I unbuckled my seat. Thundera was right next to me. Could I do it? I did it. At 7,000 feet high I slipped out of my seat and floated free. The balloon dropped below me and dwindled away. I was drifting very slowly downwards.

*– I give you more... you shall have blessed*
*lightness... you shall ride the waves with me*

The sky-whale pressed against me. She gave me even more lightness. Just a little, but enough to make all the difference. Now I could sense exactly where the waves were, rushing towards me.

*– Climb on*

I got an image of a baby whale clinging against its mother's side behind a giant flipper. I grabbed hold.

*– Watch the waves... we ride... now!*

We rose up. I'd sensed the wave coming up from below. Thundera had slipped in front of it just as it reached us, like a surfer catching a rolling wave. And now it carried us smoothly upwards. She slid off the wave and caught another one moving sideways. Once again we were carried along. Then she did a series of slides from one wave to another and we flew round in a wide circle.

*– You try now*

She shrugged me off and I somersaulted through the air. Earth and sky spun round and round as I struggled to make sense of the waves. I sensed a feeling of amusement from my giant teacher. I'll show her, I thought. I concentrated and let the upward waves steady me, just catching them long enough to keep me upright and in one place. I waited for a big one. And suddenly I was flying up like a rocket. I, Danny Peterson, earth creature, was riding the waves.

'Look Thundera!' I cried, like a kid who has just learned to ride a bike.

*– Well done Danny... you are a good little calf!*

I caught a forward wave, then a giddy downward one. I raced around like a mad thing, like any young animal who has just learned to run, swim or fly. I swooped and dived. I glided through the air. Eventually I caught a wave back to Thundera and swam up against her.

*– It is good to see you happy... I shall remember you... Danny from the shore... and what you have done for me... and my new one who comes...*

'I'll miss you too, Thundera.'

*– Let us go higher... and wait*

We rose up together. It seemed that I could ride the waves more easily than Thundera. She really needed to be out in the big ocean. Every so often she would slip behind her wave and have to catch another one. It was like surfing on a wave that's too small; you fall back and the wave goes on. But the waves were the right size for me and I could stay on them quite easily.

Other creatures were rising with us: streams of sinuous eels, flocks of tiny fishes, little wiggling crabs and the floating sponges I'd seen before. The air was warm and the waves washed around me like a relaxing massage. I began to forget the world below.

New creatures appeared from above, coming down towards us. Turtles and squid-like things, also bunches of thick-leaved plants. One of the plants brushed against my face. I was hungry and thirsty. Instinctively I caught hold of it and put it to my lips. The succulent leaves and stem tasted a bit like cucumber, a little sweet and a little salty. It was good to eat and it satisfied my thirst.

We were nearing the top of the sky-pool, where the big waves petered out. We slowed, and let the little waves hold us steady, as if we were floating. I looked up. There was something high above us, a shimmering surface stretching right across the sky. The ocean! And reaching down to us was a glinting channel of waves. The tide was coming in. The wavelets were still small, but growing bigger even as we watched. Smaller creatures were already swarming through. It was nearly time.

The channel broadened and the waves grew bigger. Thundera edged up impatiently.

*– I must go...*

'It won't be long. Only a minute.'

*– My new one comes... I must be in the ocean... with*

*my family... they are waiting*

I looked up, and saw a sight I will never forget. It was awesome. A mile above us, in that bigger sea, great shapes were gathering. Sky-whales, dozens of them. The waves grew bigger still. Thundera edged forward.

*– Lightness!... a little more lightness and I could be away...*

I don't know what it was, but at that moment something made me look down. It must have been instinct. My blood froze. Flying towards us from the depths were three sinister shapes.

'Thundera! The sharks!'

## Chapter 20 – Farewell to Thundera

The sky-whale turned in alarm. I could feel her fear and panic.

*– Danny!... I am lost!... and my new one...*

The leading shark struck her a glancing blow, spun off and circled down for another strike. I stared in horror. A hot feeling swept over me, frustration and rage. Thundera couldn't die! Not like this.

In that split second all I could think of was Thundera and the innocent infant inside her. I was right up next to her. I pressed hard against her side and willed with all my might – I take weight!

And as I sucked in, with my strange new ability, I felt my weight come out of Thundera and back into me. I fell away from her. Time seemed to stand still. In that frozen moment I saw the sky-whale surge forward, catch a wave, and begin the ride towards the safety of her home. I'd given her back the lightness she had shared with me.

But I was six miles up and about to fall a very long way. I still had a touch of lightness, for I could still see ghostly shapes, but I could not feel the waves. I was doomed. My lungs seared with cold. Earth and sky wheeled around me. I was spinning over backwards. This is it, Danny, I told myself.

But something was below me. A shark, the one who'd circled down. I struck the brute's back with both my feet.

My rage returned.

'Take weight, sucker!' I yelled, and pushed with all my might. I pushed my weight away. I pushed my weight right into that murderous shark. It spun away, floundering in sudden helplessness. But I was no longer helpless. I had lightness once again. I breathed gratefully of the warm air and surged upwards on a passing wave.

Thundera was still high above me, moving upward. And swimming down through the channel to meet her were the sky-whales. She surged up joyfully to meet them and they gathered protectively around her. Then they began to lead her up towards the ocean in the sky. A faint call came down.

    *– Farewell Danny...*

'Farewell Thundera.'

    *– I will return... we will meet again...*

'Safe journey!'

    *– Farewell...*

Then she was gone.

I glided down, zigzagging across the sky from one side to the other. I sped in circles, flew through clouds, swooped like a swallow through the air. I could see the whole county below me, tiny as a map. I focused on the moor and tiny town. Somewhere down there on the shore was my own family and my home. I could have stayed up forever, but it was time to go down once again.

I found Round Hill, a mile below, and positioned myself above it. The last few thousand feet would be wave-free, I thought, but I was light enough to drift safely down. I descended through the waves, expecting them to end while I was still high above the earth.

But then I found that the sky-whale had been mistaken, in saying the waves no longer reached the shore. On a spring tide like today's, some waves *did* reach right down to the ground. Not the proper big waves, that Thundera would need, but smaller ones that were quite adequate for little fish like me. So, using the waves, I zigzagged down and down.

Finally I came swooping in from the rear of Round Hill and skimmed across the hilltop a few feet from the ground, wondering where Alison was. There was something going on ahead of me. I could see struggling figures. They were close to the cliff edge. I zoomed nearer. It was Walker's gang!

Tucker had hold of Alison. She was struggling to get free. It looked like Walker was urging Conway to join in. I swooped nearer. Alison's eyes widened as she saw me come flying through the air. Walker had his back to me. I struck him with both feet, straight between the shoulder blades, and sent him flying. I landed in front of Alison and bounded forward as the other two swung round.

Their mouths dropped open. 'It's Peterson's ghost!' cried Conway, as I went sailing over their heads. I still had lightness, and when I'd bounded forward I hadn't realised what would happen. I flew over their heads in a slow arc and went right over the cliff. I drifted slowly down. Levity waves were bouncing up from the quarry floor and I sensed a big one coming. Suddenly I was shooting up again as though I was on an elevator. I rose up, like a ghost, past Conway and Tucker's startled faces, flew over their heads and landed behind them.

Weight flowed from the earth into my body, back to normal. I took a step forward. 'Leave her alone!'

Conway shrunk away from me, whimpering with fear. Tucker was tougher. He let go of Alison and charged towards me. I took weight, extra weight. I sucked it up from the ground and held it in for a second or two. Tucker barged into me and bounced right off again. It must have been like hitting a statue or a brick wall. He sat on the ground shaking his head. Meanwhile Walker had grabbed hold of Alison again. They were struggling near the edge.

I leaped forward. 'Leave her alone.'

He dropped her arm and stepped towards me. He swung a punch. I ducked back and he missed. Then I jumped in and struck him straight on the jaw. He went flying. I'd used no extra weight, no special powers. It was pure Danny Peterson. The kind no-one will tangle with ever again.

All this had taken just a few seconds from the time I'd come back up the cliff. And in that time I'd been aware of something happening at the edge of my vision. Someone was coming up the path to the hilltop. Suddenly I heard the sound of sirens. Two massive police motor bikes were throbbing towards us.

Alison saw them too. 'Dad! They attacked me! Danny saved me.'

Inspector Day swung off the leading bike. 'I know. I saw them. Well done, Danny.'

I fixed Conway with my eyes. ' You must tell Inspector Day about Jason Blant. Do you understand?'

The poor sod nodded fearfully. He would do anything I told him. 'It wasn't me,' he muttered. 'It was them two what did it.'

'Shut up, you fool!' snarled Walker.

Inspector Day pricked up his ears. The case was still open. 'Jason Blant? I think you three should come along with me.'

They were handcuffed and Inspector Day radioed for a van to take them away.

I went up to Alison. 'Are you alright?'

'I'm alright now, Danny. You were fantastic.'

She put her arms round my neck and pulled me close. 'Do you know what Thundera said to me?' she whispered. 'She said I must be glad to have a mate like you.'

'Would you really like to be my mate?'

'Course I would!'

# Chapter 21 – Up, up and away

What happened back on the ground the next few days was almost as surreal as our adventures in the sky. The next morning we had to see the headmaster in his office. I tapped on his door and pushed it open.

'Come in, come in,' he said, springing up. 'Have a seat. Here's one for you, Alison.' He carried a chair over for her.

Something was odd here. Usually kids have to stand to attention in front of him while he sits behind his big desk like a judge. But today Mr Grayson sat beside us like an oily chat show host.

'How are you two feeling this morning?' he asked sympathetically.

'Fine thanks.'

'Um, Danny, Alison, as you know we have a very strict policy about bullying at this school. Violence or intimidation are not tolerated.' He looked at me warily. 'I know, Danny, certain things have happened and it's a police matter now, but tell me, did anything happen to you here on the premises?'

'No sir, not at school.' That's what he wanted to hear, and there was no point telling him about the odd kick in the shin. Not anymore.

'And you Alison?'

She shook her head. 'No sir.'

He smiled with relief. 'That's good. Naturally we would

take firm action if anything happened here. What I'll do is write a letter confirming what you've said. Just for the record.'

That was it. Everyone assumed we'd gone missing because of Walker. They didn't even ask us. When we got outside the office we couldn't stop laughing. Walker had given us the perfect excuse, without us even trying. We didn't have to explain anything.

Alison had told her father about me being kidnapped, and the plot to throw me off the cliff. The thugs thought I knew about Jason Blant's 'accident', and that was the motive. It was just like those movies where the bad guys try to bump off the witness. There was even a video recording of them hassling me at the car park.

Everyone had been puzzled by our behaviour. They couldn't understand it. People don't like mysteries, so when the Walker gang explanation popped up they were happy to accept it. If you think about it, there were still a lot of unanswered questions, but that didn't seem to matter. No-one asked us. No-one found out about the balloon, or our rides through the air, and we never had to explain about the sky-whale or the ocean in the sky.

Conway sang like a canary. He told the police what the gang had done to Jason Blant, and lots of other things as well. He became the witness that Walker had been so careful to avoid. Other victims of the gang came forward to add to the charges. Walker and Tucker were sent away for a very long time. I doubt if we'll ever see them again.

I became a welcome guest at the Day's and even had some good conversations with her father. It helped that I could show him how to do stuff on his computer.

We retrieved our tent and found the balloon alright. It came to earth a mile beyond our little campsite. For the next few days we spent the afternoons together on the moor and up the hill, while the spring tide lasted. How did we know the tide was there? We knew because we could see the waves round the hill. And we could see the waves because we had lightness. That was Thundera's gift to us. We can give weight now. We can gain lightness. We can ride the waves.

Thundera had taught Alison how to give and take weight that day they'd spent so much time together. I had found it hard to learn at first, but somehow on that final day it came to me too. I think it was that last desperate moment when the sharks attacked that I finally learned to do it for myself.

And we didn't have to be up in the air to do it. Back on Round Hill we found that we had an urge to push our weight away, to become light again. Alison reckons it's a latent instinct; something that all creatures could do if only they knew how.

We had to practice at first, and figure out how to get going. When we're on the ground we can push our weight out into the earth and hold it for a couple of seconds. But the pressure's enormous and the weight comes flooding back.

So what we do is jump onto a rising wave the moment we get light. Once we're in the air there's nowhere else for the lightness to go, nothing to give us back our weight. Lightness and weight. They both seem real things to me, though you may think one is just the absence of the other.

Now, for a few days each month, when the tide is in and the sky-pool reaches down to the shore, we go up Round Hill to ride the waves. When the waves touch the earth we simply leap onto one, and away we go. We can fly up high into the sky as easy as anything. Granddad was right all along, you *can* fall towards the clouds.

We make the most of the special time. The waves spread out around the hill, and quite a lot of the moor is in contact with them. We've seen other creatures coming and going too; bugs and things, turning invisible and hopping onto the waves just like us. We can see them clearly now of course, since we become nearly invisible too.

It's best to go quite high up, near the top of the pool. The waves are stronger and also we don't lose lightness. Closer to the earth we can feel the heaviness seeping in after a time, and we begin to struggle and sink. Just like poor Thundera. How frightened she must have been.

Sometimes we float and fly all day, five or six miles up. The air is always warm. There is plenty of juicy food floating around, and we've discovered what's good to eat. You don't really need anything up there. Even clothes seem unnecessary and we often wear just our swimsuits. It seems right, somehow. We could live up there, with food to eat and the waves to wash us clean.

Sometimes we spend the night up in the sky. We swim all the way to the top of the waves and lie together, just floating, looking at the stars. We hold each other and the waves rock us gently and it gets as perfect as it can be.

At times I wonder where we really belong. Close to earth or in the sky. On the shore or in the waves. All I know is that the whales were very wise to venture into the high seas all those centuries ago.

Several months have passed since we first helped the sky-whale. The channel to the ocean is getting wider with each spring tide that comes, and the waves are getting stronger. Already smaller creatures are swimming to and fro. Soon we'll be able to swim up to the ocean ourselves. We both feel the urge to go further into the deep. But we shall wait for the sky-whales to return before we do.

And then, who knows? As the stars drift through the heavens and the earth turns far below, perhaps we shall journey with the sky-whales, and swim away across the skies.

THE END

Did you enjoy this story?
Why not visit the author's website and
say what you think of it.

Also, see what's coming next!

www.pjmarsden.com